The Jack-o-Lantern Box

The Jack-o-Lantern Box

Karen Joan Kohoutek

Skull and Book Press
Fargo, ND

ISBN: 978-0-578-12842-9

Skull and Book Press, Fargo, North Dakota 58103

For Kathy and Jeanie.

Part One

Suggestions for Hallowe'en

When Jessy got to school on the first of October, her best friend Karma asked right away, "Have you started the Halloween story?"

"Not yet," Jessy said. "I'm thinking of something different."

"What kind of different?"

"I don't know. That's what's different about it."

Karma nodded, looking sage.

"There's so many spooky elements. It's hard to pick one," Jessy went on. "First I thought it might be about vampires. But today I've been thinking about ghosts. So I just don't know yet."

Karma's eyes got a little excited.

"Vampires are great," she said.

"I know," Jessy agreed.

Jessy and Karma had been best friends since they were in kindergarten, and it seemed like they should have run out of things to talk about, but they never had. They updated each other every day before school, and at recess, and they took turns going over to each other's houses most days after school.

They had other friends too, but most of them weren't as much fun. They always wanted to do things like play with baby dolls, which Jessy thought was even more boring than school. The last time she played dolls with anyone, she pretended her husband was a famous rock star who got killed in a plane crash. That was so dramatic that everybody wanted to kill off their pretend husbands. But they kept on changing their dolls' diapers, so they were still crazy.

"I saw this movie once, and the vampire was kind of cute," Karma went on.

"Gross!"

"But he was," Karma said, with conviction.

Jessy stared at her. "Vampires drink blood out of people's necks."

"I know that." Karma was nonchalant. "But so what?"

"Have you ever tasted blood?"

They thought about it for a second. Jessy thought about chewing her fingernails, and the scratchy skin around them, and how they'd bleed if she pulled on them the wrong way. Then she'd suck the blood out, hoping they'd heal up fast, so her mom wouldn't notice how gross and raw they looked. Her mom was always bugging her about her cuticles.

The blood didn't taste good; it had a strange quality, kind of -- shiny in her mouth. But she had swallowed it herself, so maybe she should be nicer about the vampires and their grossness.

"Of course vampires are icky," Karma said. "But that doesn't mean they couldn't be cute. A guy can be cute even if you don't like him, because it's just his face. And cuteness can be … capricious."

"I guess that's true," Jessy said. "But just think. What if you met a cute guy, and then he turned out to be a vampire. What would you do?"

"It would depend on if he was going to drink my blood," Karma said.

"You're so practical."

That night, when her parents were in the living room watching TV, she asked, "Mom, can I get out the Jack-o-Lantern Box this week?"

"It's too early," her mom said, without even considering it.

"It's not too early."

"You need to wait until it gets closer to Halloween. Otherwise, by the time it gets here, it won't even be fun anymore."

"That's not true," she exclaimed. The very idea that she could get tired of Halloween was ridiculous.

"You're just going to have to wait."

"Mom …"

"That's all I'm going to say." She didn't even look away from the television while she was talking.

Jessy clomped up the stairs to her room.

"Turn on the light when you go up the stairs," her mom yelled. So Jessy went up the stairs in the dark, and then, when she got to the top, she switched the light on.

None of the bedroom doors ever got closed all the way, just most of the way, or else they'd stick shut. "Humidity," her mom said. When she went to bed, Jessy left hers so the edge of the door and the edge of the frame were just barely touching. It was easier to hear the TV that way, and if their cat, Cupcake, wanted to come in, she could push it open with the top of her head.

Her sister Twyla had hers wedged close to shut, leaving a faint line of visible light in the crack. Their mom always said she was sulking in her room. For once, Jessy could understand what there was to sulk about. She pushed her own door open, and then shut it behind her, as much as she dared.

Right inside was a small desk with some open shelves, that had come from her dad's antiquing. She had begged to keep it in her room; she needed a desk, to work on her stories, like a real writer. But all she ever did was pile papers and stuff on it. It was just like how her grandma kept buying her fancy blank books, and once an official diary, with a tiny key, but they just didn't feel comfortable. Instead she'd grab a pen and her plain notebook, like the ones she used every day at school, and sit on the bed while she was writing.

The last two Halloweens, the stories had been about a couple of girls -- obviously her and Karma with made-up names -- who thought they were witches. Cupcake, and Karma's Yorkshire terrier, George, were also in the stories, with their real names, and they were the ones who actually had the magic powers, even though the witches didn't realize it. Jessy had illustrated them, too, with crayon drawings of George and Cupcake in capes and pointed hats, stirring a cauldron with ladles in their cartoon paws.

The first year, the story had been really short, just scenes of the girls making potions, and then flying over the town on their broomsticks, nearly hitting the roof of the JC Penney's store. There was a vague plot about somebody who had put a curse on Jessy and Karma's characters, and Cupcake and George had to save the day. It didn't make a lot of sense, but Karma had really liked that she made little shaggy George so heroic.

Last year, the story was much more elaborate, and it had taken Jessy a lot longer than a story usually took her to write. In it, all their friends' pets met in a Sabbat on the edge of town, in a field out behind Karma's parents' house. They stood in a circle, on their hind legs, wearing the traditional witches' hats and long flowing gowns, and did magical battle with a group of mean pets, who belonged to nasty kids.

She'd been really proud of one of the plot twists: when George and Cupcake made up a magic potion, they would lick it into their fur. Then the magic transferred to whoever petted them. Sometimes she still thought about that when she was petting Cupcake, the soft fat kitty plopped on her side and purring.

This year, though, she was determined to write a story that was more grown up.

Let's see, she thought. What do I know about vampires?

It wasn't much, really. She had a picture in her mind, like out of a black and white movie, and it was full of billowing fog. It's not as if the vampires actually caused the fog, but they were clearly associated in her mind. Then she imagined a cemetery at night, and someone walking, in old-fashioned clothes. But she didn't know what would happen next.

She wrote "If I was a vampire" in her notebook. But she knew she'd never be a vampire, so that wasn't much help.

Then underneath she added the phrase, "If I was a ghost." Somehow it was easier to imagine being a ghost, although she skipped right over the part about dying.

Jessy started picturing a scene of ghosts all over town, maybe just walking down the street, a whole parade of them. It was puzzling, though -- she didn't know what the ghosts would actually do. Where did they go when they weren't busy haunting people? Were they just hanging around?

It was hard to think of what they'd do, since she couldn't imagine what it would be like to be dead. It all seemed so complicated. Did they have bodies, that you could touch? Or were they something misty and vague, like the fog? What would you want, if you weren't even alive anymore?

In the movies, it seemed like you only became a ghost if you hadn't been very nice when you were alive. Or maybe you wanted something, like there was a message you wanted to pass on. She couldn't think of anything she'd need to say so urgently that she'd come all the way back from the grave.

There was a knock at her door.

"Who is it?" she called. The door pushed open, rasping slightly, and Twyla was standing there, slouched.

"Did you go in my room?" she demanded.

"No, and I didn't say you could come in," Jessy said.

Funny that vampires could rise up from their coffins, right through the dirt, and they still couldn't enter her room if she didn't want them to. But she couldn't keep her stupid sister out.

"Don't be a brat."

"You're the brat," Jessy replied.

"Just answer the question."

Jessy glared at her.

"Why would I go in your room?" she asked, even though there were a million reasons to go into her sister's room. She snuck in there to listen to records all the time.

"Because you're a snoop," Twyla said.

"I am not a snoop."

That wasn't totally true either. She knew where Twyla had hidden a bottle of Boone's Farm Strawberry Wine, in an old purse in her closet, but that just made Jessy more indignant.

"Like you'd admit it if you were snooping," Twyla went on.

"Well I didn't, so leave me alone."

"Well, if it wasn't you, it must have been Mom."

Music was flowing into the hallway, between the doors. Jessy knew every record that Twyla had, and all the flip sides, but this must be something new. She really wanted to ask what it was, but she couldn't back down.

There was a pause.

"You think Mom snoops in your room?" Jessy asked then.

"I fixed my drawer so I could tell if it had been opened. When I got home, I noticed right away."

Jessy immediately wondered about the stuff she had hidden in her own closet, mostly paperbacks with "good parts." And she had plenty of notebooks where she'd written about boys, and even some attempts at a romance novel that had gotten pretty steamy, by her standards. Right now, their mom was probably worrying more about Twyla, but if she looked through Twyla's stuff, maybe Jessy wasn't safe either.

****

Some autumn days were just perfect, still warm enough to play outside, but with occasional cool wind, just to remind you that Halloween was coming. Jessy didn't want to waste a day when it wasn't raining, or cold, or starting to snow, and it was really annoying that she had to go to school.

At least in the fall, there was hope that the teachers might do something interesting, since they were getting into the season too. Whether it was making spider webs or collecting autumn leaves, every day with Halloween in it was a good day.

If they were lucky, there'd be a few days during Reading class when the teacher would read something scary to the class. The teachers were usually in the middle of a book, just like Jessy herself was, but they read them a lot slower, part of a chapter, a couple of times a week. It had been awful last year when the teacher read *Charlotte's Web*, and everyone had to sit silently in their desks and pretend they didn't want to cry. But you couldn't cry in class, no matter what, because no one would let you forget it. That was the law.

It was still warm enough to go to the playground for recess. Kids pushed and shoved as they lined up in the tiled hallway, past all the closed classroom doors, deceptively calm and quiet with their frosted glass windows, already covered with red construction paper leaves, and brown paper acorns.

The school had one brick wall that was covered with vines, and they passed it on the way to the playground. The vines were already so autumn red that it looked like the wall was leaking blood. That made Jessy think about real blood streaming down the brick, disguised by the vines, and pooling on the grass below. Veins behind the vines, she thought, and then she thought it really hard, over and over, hoping that she'd remember the phrase to write it down when they got back to class.

At the playground, Jessy and her friends sat on the parallel bars. Each side had a ladder made of metal rungs. Some kids called it the monkey bars, but that was a different structure, a whole complex of climbing bars, several sections square and tall, like the frame of a building, that you could climb through, inside and out.

On the parallel bars, when you got to the top, you could walk across it, but with your hands, since it was high enough that your feet wouldn't touch the ground. That was where they did the chicken fighting. Two contestants would start on opposite sides. You put your hands on the bars, which felt like rough metal pipes, and stretched your legs behind you, steadied on the ladder. When someone yelled "Go," you'd swing toward each other, moving with your hands to meet in the middle, and swinging your legs, trying to knock the other kid to the ground.

When teachers were around, though, all you could do was climb up it, hook your hands on the bars, and swing across. It was sort of like the dive bombing. To do that, you'd just swing on the swing set, until you got as high as you could possibly go. Then, when you were sure you couldn't get any higher, you'd launch and jump right off. It seemed kind of scary the first time, but when you didn't get hurt, you just wanted to try it again.

Sometimes they'd get into a synchronized dive bombing. There'd be a signal, and they'd all jump together. Or they'd all jump in shifts, first one swinger, then the next. That was dangerous, though, because it took longer, and that increased the chance that a teacher would see them. Once Gary, a kid in her class, did the first round of a staggered jump, and when he got caught, he had to sit in the back of the room for the rest of the day.

Somewhere a kid had probably banged his head and died from jumping off a swing, but they'd never heard of anybody. Jessy had done it a million times.

"A googolplex," Karma would correct her.

While they talked on the chicken-fighting bars, someone would occasionally drop down over the side, hanging upside down, attached by the knees.

"You should never play with a Ouija board," Corey had been saying. "Because you never know what spirits are talking to you."

"Jessy has a Ouija board," Karma said, which caused a buzz.

"It's no big deal," Jessy said. "We play with it all the time."

"Does it tell you things?" Allison said.

"Yeah, but it's kind of vague about it."

"If you start talking to spirits, they're going to come and haunt you," Corey insisted. "That's what my Grandma says."

"My cousin told me how she went to this haunted house once," Allison put in.

"A real one? With a ghost?" they clamored.

"No, the ones you walk through, and people try to scare you. Like a funhouse at the carnival."

When they went to the county fair every summer, there had never been a funhouse, but they'd all seen them in movies and TV shows.

"It was out in the country, by this place where they have hayrides."

"I wish we had something like that here," Jessy said, wistful.

"Or maybe a real haunted house," Karma added.

"We do have a real haunted house," Corey said.

"Where?"

Corey looked abashed.

"You know. The Murder House."

The Murder House was supposed to be haunted, except that nobody had ever seen a ghost there. It still seemed awfully creepy, since none of the kids in the neighborhood could remember anyone living in it. The grass got mowed, and the leaves got raked, but nobody was ever seen going in or out.

"It's not a Murder House," Jessy said. "That's just a story."

"There was too a murder," Allison said. "It was a long time ago. They were the richest family in town, and one night, while they were sleeping, the whole family was killed. And they never found the weapon!" Every word was underlined in her voice.

"It sure looks haunted," Corey said. Which nobody could argue with.

****

"I'm home," Jessy hollered into the space just inside the door. There was a clump of sound from the other room, and her mom popped her head around the corner.

"There's brownies in the kitchen," she said. "Only one."

"Karma's here."

"That's fine."

They went into the kitchen and took out little plates from the cupboard, cut out raggedy-edged chocolate squares, and then plunked the brownies onto their plates. They were delicious.

"How was school?" her mom said, appearing in the doorway.

"Fine."

"Anything new going on?"

There never was, so Jessy just shrugged.

"Your sister isn't outside, is she?"

The window in the kitchen looked plainly out onto the yard. Unless she was crouched hiding behind the overgrown rose bush, it was obvious that Twyla wasn't there.

"I didn't see her," Jessy said.

"Mmm." Her mom made a non-committal noise and left the kitchen.

"My mom has a new *Redbook*," Jessy said then.

"Really?" Karma asked. "I hope there's a quiz."

They loved *Redbook*, because it was the raciest of the women's magazines. Every year they had a big quiz asking the readers about their sex lives, and it had been much more informative than most of the paperbacks in Jessy's stash, which were more suggestive, and tended to go vague right when they really needed the details.

After the brownies, they went upstairs to Jessy's room.

"It's not fair that she won't let me get out the Jack-o-Lantern Box," Jessy complained. "We could get a head start on the decorating."

"We can always make some new decorations," Karma suggested.

They hauled out a carton filled with scissors and glue and all the other craft supplies, and spread them out on the floor. There was a whole pack of construction paper, with different colors, and one that was nothing but black, along with a wad of paper sheets that were already partially used, leaving them full of strange holes, or cut into odd rectangles. A lot of the supplies used to be Twyla's, but she had cleared all that stuff out of her room.

"I can use my new colors," Jessy said.

She had nagged her mom mercilessly for them when the school year started. They weren't the official crayons on the official list, which was only the regular 64-count pack. Her mom would never let her get the super-giant pack, with all the extra colors, because they weren't necessary for her classes, and besides, they were expensive. It's true, the kids with the big crayon boxes did seem like show-offs, so maybe her mom had a point.

This packet of crayons was totally different, though, a smaller batch of colors that were supposed to be fluorescent.

"You can't be drawing the grass neon-green," her mom had said.

"Why not?"

"The grass is supposed to be grass-green."

That seemed like a very limited view of the world. Finally her mom had agreed to let her buy them, so long as she didn't bring them to school.

Jessy sat on the floor, legs crossed in the lotus position, and opened the glossy cardboard edge of the crayon package. The colors were pastel, but bright, not the pale, washed-out colors she thought of as pastel, like outfits she'd have to wear to church on Easter Sunday. She ran her finger along the tops.

"There's a lot of black construction paper left," Karma said, flipping through the paper book.

"Yeah. So, what should we make?"

They thought for a minute.

"Well," Jessy said. "We have bats and cats and owls and stuff in the Jack-o-Lantern Box."

"Do you have the patterns?"

The other decorations had been made with card stock patterns, that Jessy's mom had gotten from a magazine. They traced around the shapes, onto the construction paper, then cut them out.

"The patterns are in the box, too."

"Well, we could make new patterns, but I can't draw long-hand."

"Yes, you can," Jessy said. "You can draw really good."

"There's orange paper, too," Karma added. "We could start with some jack-o-lanterns. They're easy."

"And we can make the eyes and noses and mouths out of the black paper scraps."

"What about the colors?"

"We're just going to have to try and draw some pictures," Jessy said. "Some scenes."

They each grabbed a book to use as a smooth surface, and spread a sheet of plain white typing paper on it. Karma started sketching in pencil before she colored. Jessy grabbed a pink crayon and drew a big blobby oblong. Kind of like a circle, but she wasn't worried about how it looked, if it was really a circle or not. Then she filled in the circle with more pink, and used the green and the blue -- which was a disappointing shade, kind of watery -- to give the shape big, bulbous eyes.

The colors were paler on paper than they looked in the box, and it was impossible to get the colors very dark, even when she went over and over them. Still, they gave everything an eerie quality, as if they might glow in the dark.

"Weird," Karma said, looking over at what she'd done.

"What are you drawing?" Jessy asked.

"I'm trying an owl," she said. "Maybe I'll use the orange."

"That would look nice."

Karma's concentrated really hard on her owl, staring at the paper, and muttering how the crayon wasn't doing what she wanted it to do.

After awhile they stopped and inspected their work. The owl looked great, filling the page with its big staring eyes, and detailed feathers on its body, brown and orange. Little hooky feet clutched onto the tree branch it sat on. Jessy's drawing was finally identifiable as a spider, with long, hairy tentacle legs, and behind it, an uneven red web.

They both tried to draw skulls, but they couldn't make the shapes right. So Jessy started drawing a witch's head, with long stringy orange hair and a green warty face. The colors were perfect for that, and it didn't matter if the face was off-balance. Karma began an elaborate landscape, starting with a green horizontal line on the bottom of the paper. She drew some thin spindly trees and some oval-headed tombstones, and put a sliver of moon in the sky. In the sky-space behind the moon, she carefully filled in a thin violet color.

"That's beautiful," Jessy said. It was. She wanted to live in that picture.

"Where are we going to hang them up?" Karma asked.

"All over," Jessy said.

They had some time before Karma's dad would be coming to pick her up. Jessy's parents were talking in the kitchen, and they ignored her when she went in to dig the Scotch tape out of the junk drawer. Then she and Karma picked spots to tape up their masterpieces, on the walls in the living room and the dining room.

When that was done, they went outside and sat on the steps. It was already starting to get darkish early in the day. A slight breeze rustled the leaves.

"We have quiz in Reading tomorrow, don't we?" Karma said.

"Yeah." That meant it wasn't going to be a fun class. The teachers didn't seem to like the quizzes and tests any more than the kids did.

Down the block, they could see Twyla coming down the sidewalk. She was walking with a boy that Jessy didn't recognize. They were walking really close together, and when they got a little nearer, Jessy could see that he had his hand hooked around the loop on the front of her jeans.

Twyla had a boyfriend for a while, but they hadn't seen him around in a long time. Jessy didn't know if they'd had a fight or broken up, or if it was just a coincidence.

"Hey," Twyla called when they got in heying distance of the house. "Whatcha doing?"

"We've just been playing," Jessy said.

Twyla plunked down on top of the picnic table, between the steps and the cellar door. The guy just stood next to her, like he wasn't sure what to do.

"Cool," she said.

"I gotta go," the guy said.

"Yeah." She tilted her head back a little, and he leaned down and they kissed, hard, like they were really concentrating. If their mom or dad looked out the kitchen window right then, they could see the whole thing. Twyla didn't seem to care at all, but the idea made Jessy very nervous.

"See you tomorrow," the guy said, and grinned. He raised his hand in a casual acknowledgement of Jessy and Karma as he left.

"Who's that?" Jessy asked.

"A friend." Twyla shrugged, and fiddled in the breast pocket of her jean jacket. She buttoned the unbuttoned one, and checked the other. She seemed to be holding something small, but then she quickly slipped her hand in the pocket of her jeans. Sleight of hand.

"So what have you been playing?"

"We've been drawing and stuff," Jessy told her. Then, "Mom was looking for you before."

"I wasn't doing anything."

"You were doing something."

Twyla gave her a look. "Don't be a brat."

"I'm not," Jessy said. "It's logic."

"I was just hanging out. There's no law against that. Not yet."

They all sat in silence for a minute.

"They're talking about a big bonfire down at the skating rink next weekend," Twyla said suddenly. She usually updated them on the doings of the high school kids, like it was a TV show they were all watching. "After the football game."

"Will you go?"

"Well, maybe. It depends on if there's anything else going on. There'll probably be some parties. Someone should be getting a keg."

High school sounded very glamorous to Jessy. It was always a party, always a drama. Elementary school was really boring.

"We had to play the recorders today," she said.

"Oh, I hated the recorder!" Twyla said. "They still do that?"

"Yeah."

"That's no way to teach music." Then, "You know Mike?"

"Mike who?"

"He was just here."

"Oh, that guy," Jessy said, like it was a matter of no concern.

"He's going to teach me to play the guitar."

"Really?" Both Jessy and Karma got kind of excited at that. Then, "Jinx," they both said, and fast as they could, "One two three four five six seven eight nine ten." And Karma punched her in the arm.

"He's going to let me use his old acoustic guitar, to practice on."

Jessy really couldn't picture her playing an acoustic guitar, like she was Joan Baez or something. It was like Twyla could read her mind.

"It's not what I'd pick, but it's free, and it'll be a lot quieter to practice on."

"That's true," Jessy agreed.

"My brother has an old electric guitar that he left in the garage," Karma said. Everyone they knew had a crush on her brother Todd, who was even older than Twyla, and had gone off to college.

"That's right. He and Gene Sorensen had that band," Twyla said. She gave a snorting laugh.

"What's funny?" Jessy asked.

"Nothing." She still looked amused though. "Maybe someday you guys will start a band."

Jessy and Karma looked at each other. What a thought. Todd had played a couple of parties, and once they did a school dance, but that had been the end of their career. Then there was the sister of another girl in their grade, someone who was the acoustic guitar type. She dropped out of school to join a traveling band of Jesus Freaks who played Christian folk music. That was really, truly glamorous, more than they could imagine.

The sky was starting to get darker. It seemed like they should be getting called in to eat, or that Karma's dad should be showing up any second. Leaves skittered suggestively on the sidewalk.

"Do you remember when they used to have the bonfires at Grandma's old farm?" Twyla asked, a dreamy look on her face.

"I don't know." Jessy searched her mind.

Before she went into the nursing home, their Grandma had lived on the old farm, although she hadn't actually planted anything, or kept animals, in years. Behind the house, before you hit the scrubby scruff of woods, were some old run-down farm buildings, the paint long gone, everything a decaying grey. And there was a circle of scorched ground where they used to burn garbage, and a few big heavy metal drums of garbage cans, all of it surrounded by trees. Jessy remembered a weeping willow somewhere nearby, and a patch of evergreen trees, a silvery flicker of birches behind them.

"They used to burn garbage behind the old barn," Twyla went on. "And there were marks on the ground, where they obviously used to burn bigger stuff, like when they had cut down a lot of branches."

"I remember that," Jessy said.

"Well, one night when we staying there, one summer, I woke up in the middle of the night, and I could smell something burning. So I sat up, kind of worried, thinking there was a fire. I got out of bed and tiptoed into the hallway. And Gordon was already out there, in his pajamas." Gordon was their cousin, a year older than Twyla. "I asked what he was doing up, and he said he could see something burning out his window. We were sleeping in the bedroom on the side of the house facing toward the highway, remember?"

Jessy did. They always slept in that room.

"And the boys were in one of the rooms across the hall. Anyway, he said he could see something red out in the woods. The house was quiet, just totally silent, like you weren't even breathing. And it was dark, just a little light from the window in the stairwell. It was spooky."

Jessy and Twyla were hanging on her every word.

"So we found our shoes and we tiptoed outside. It was kind of eerie, out there in the country, because there was no one around. No street lights, no house across the street, you know? It was just … us. In the dark. And the old buildings were all dark and empty and falling apart. Gordon was right. I could see the flicker of red through the trees. We just walked toward the glow. Every crack that the ground made underneath our feet sounded just thunderously loud."

The wind seemed to pick up a little bit. Jessy shivered. She should have worn her jacket, but she hadn't, just because her mom would have told her to put it on.

"When we got closer, we could tell there were people out by the garbage pit. We went around the corner of the old barn, and peered into the clearing. You remember there was that a kind of semicircle

20

of trees around it? So it was open on the one side, and on the other, a ring of trees, like a screen from the sky. There was a huge fire burning in a patch on the ground, and they were all standing around the flames."

"Who?" Jessy demanded.

"It took a minute for my eyes to adjust to the light, but then I realized it was Mom and Dad and Aunt Bonita and Uncle Jerry, and then some other people I didn't recognize. Neighbors, maybe."

"What were they doing?" Karma asked.

"They were standing there, silent. Kind of swaying, making dark shadows against the fire. Then somebody I didn't recognize lifted his hands above his head, and they started swaying faster, and they were kind of, I don't know how to describe it." She pondered. "Chanting."

"Chanting?"

"They were mumbling, and saying something, but it didn't make any sense to me. They started moving faster, like they were dancing, standing in place and shaking. And the chanting got louder and louder, and then I was getting really scared. I didn't know what was going to happen. It looked like they were totally out of control. Then the leader guy raised his hands again, and he said some word, that wasn't in English. And Mom and Aunt Bonita and the other women took off their tops."

"What?"

"They kind of writhed, and they took off their shirts, and they threw them into the fire."

"All of them?"

"All of the women were standing there, dancing in front of the fire, just wearing their bras."

"What were they doing?" Karma asked, her voice low.

"I don't know. I didn't really understand what I was seeing. Aunt Bonita started dancing really crazy, and she was panting for breath, and then she just – tore her bra off, in this crazy gesture, and she threw the bra in the bonfire too. When that happened, the flames echoing off her skin, Gordon just gasped out loud."

Jessy and Karma both gasped too.

"He gasped out loud, and they stopped, and turned to look at us."

Jessy's whole body was tense.

"What happened?"

"I just remember some kind of commotion. The group seemed to kind of break up, and Mom and Aunt Bonita came over to us, and she was wearing a shirt."

"How did that happen?"

"I think Uncle Jerry must have given it to her, but I don't know. Then in the morning, I woke up in bed, and you were asleep. I tried to ask Mom later what had happened, and she said I'd had a dream."

"Do you think it was a dream?" Jessy asked.

"The thing is, it seemed like a dream. It seems more like a dream than like something that really happened. But when I woke up, I could smell the smoke on my hair, and on my pajamas. It was all oily smoky, just like a bonfire. But the grown-ups acted like nothing had happened."

"What do you think did happen?" Karma asked.

Twyla leaned over toward them, and her voice got really, really quiet.

"I think they were witches," she said.

Jessy and Karma sat there, stone silent.

Suddenly there was a bang on the screen door.

"Dinner's ready!" their Mom called in the dinner-bell voice. Then, in a normal speaking tone, "Karma, you better call your folks."

Twyla darted up and went into the house, their mom saying, "Nice of you to join us."

Jessy and Karma half-dashed inside too. Karma called her mom, who said her dad was on his way. She'd barely put the phone down when they saw his car pull up. Jessy walked back out to the front steps with her.

"She was making that up, wasn't she?" Karma asked.

"She had to have been," Jessy said. "If she'd seen something that crazy, she would have told me about it before now."

"I knew she was making it up," Karma said.

"Me too."

But they both still sounded worried.

At dinner, their mom waited until everyone was eating, and then she said, "I see we have some new art work in the house."

"I like it," Twyla said. "Very original."

"Thanks," Jessy said.

"Yeah. I've never seen a pink spider before. Or a spider with antennae."

Jessy glared at her. "You're not an expert on spiders."

Their mom looked at them, amused. "I'm not sure it's exactly the decorating scheme I have in mind," she went on. "And you know you need permission before you start taping things up on the walls."

"It's only until Halloween," Jessy said.

Their mom sighed.

"The colors are a little garish," she muttered.

"Oh, go ahead," her dad put in. "Let her have her fun."

"You're not the one who's going to have to clean off the tape marks."

****

Over the weekend, her dad went to run an errand. It wasn't supposed to take very long, so her mom fidgeted around the house, and finally, sick of waiting, she went out for groceries by herself. When she came home, Jessy helped her take stuff out of the crackling paper bags.

"Pineapple-coconut juice?" she said, looking at a tall curved bottle. It was white like milk, but almost see-through.

"It's something new," her mom said.

When the bags were empty, Jessy smoothed them out and folded them carefully, before tucking them into the spot between the refrigerator and the wall. She had a lot of uses for good paper bags this time of year. Then she tried a little glass of the pineapple-coconut juice. It seemed thicker than milk, but somehow thinner at the same time. The taste made her think of the time she and Twyla had sprawled out on the grass in the summer, trying to imagine a color they'd never seen. Because how would they know what it was like, if they'd never seen it?

If I'm going to be a writer, she thought, I have to figure out how to describe something like that. It wasn't all describing cobwebs in the doorways of haunted houses. The characters had to live places, and do things, and eat things. That was really the hard part, even though that seemed totally backward.

When her dad came in the door, he was carrying a cardboard box with a dirty cover. Her mom instinctively looked horrified, but when they went out to help him unload the car, she tried to put on a cheerful expression.

"What do you have there?" she said. Jessy could hear the needly sound in her voice, but her dad didn't seem to notice.

"Joe Storvig had a couple of pieces to give me," he said. "But he wanted to get rid of it all as a bunch. I said I'd haul it away, and he was happy to give them to me for free."

Jessy knew some of the Storvig kids. There were a bunch of boys; one was in Twyla's grade, and Jessy had played intramural basketball with one who was a year younger than she was.

"What are you going to do with all this stuff?" her mom said.

"I can sort through it, and see if there's anything worth saving. If there isn't, I can bring it to the dump."

"You still have stuff in the garage to take to the dump."

"Oh, that's hardly enough to make it worth a trip."

Jessy didn't know why it bothered her mom, since she never went out to the garage. Her dad went into the garage and got the car, and then he pulled around in front of the house to them pick up, whenever they went anywhere. Since her mom never even saw the inside, why did she even think about it? But she obviously did.

"I'll have this all out in a couple of days," he said. Her mom looked skeptical. "I will. I promise." He looked over at Jessy.

"Here you go," he called. "Grab a box." He found one that wasn't too heavy for her to carry. The flaps were crossed on the top, but starting to separate. It looked like there were papers inside.

"Those boxes are going to be full of spiders," her mom said. "Maybe mice."

They set the boxes down in a stack in the dining room.

"Want to see what I got?" he asked.

"Sure," Jessy said.

"And the mice are going to have baby mice all over this house," her mom continued, to no one.

It was another box, but long and wooden; something real, not cardboard. He pulled on a lever and a top came up. Then he pulled at something, and a kind of shallow drawer opened up, separated into a row of little crannies.

"It's a portable desk," he said. He ran his finger around a circle that was cut into the upper right hand of the surface. "See, this is where you'd put your ink bottle."

Jessy touched the long groove underneath, where a fountain pen would go.

"It's like the *Little House on the Prairie* books," she said.

"I'm going to strip all this off, and sand it down and repaint it. It's going to look great."

Their mom had to help him lift an old dresser out of the car, complaining the whole time. It came with a big mirror that was supposed to be attached but wasn't, the glass mottling into dark patches. Jessy was thrilled that their dad opened up the cellar door, which protruded from the house, like it was erupting out of the ground. That was always such an event, like the rare times when they got to light the old kerosene lamps. Dried leaves curled up in the corners of the cement steps, all the way down into the basement, where the workshop was.

Besides all the furniture their dad was working on, there was a wall of preserves and canned goods, lined up on rough wooden board shelves, and then shiny metal shelves filled with toilet paper and paper towels and everything their mom was afraid they'd run out of. Nothing was ever going to catch her by surprise.

The biggest part of the basement was full of their dad's workroom, where he spent most of his time. A bunch of scary-looking tools hung on pegboard, over an old rusty cupboard that leaned against the wall, full of jars, and cans of paint and finish, and mysterious oily smelly liquids. Her dad wanted to start some kind of business refinishing furniture, and he kept buying old wooden pieces at auction sales. Jessy and Twyla were absolutely forbidden from going in there, even though they always had to help him wrestle stuff down the stairs.

Twyla had already started digging through the boxes, and she pulled something out of a bigger carton.

"Look at this," she said. It was a rolled-up window shade, made of heavy paper.

"There's some real junk in here, isn't there?" their dad said.

"Can we have it?"

"What for?"

"I don't know. We can do something with it."

Jessy came over and kneeled on her knees. She wasn't sure she was part of Twyla's "we," but it was worth looking into. Twyla handed her the roll. The texture of the screen was like linen, and it was kind of linen-colored, slightly darkened. Not exactly yellowed, but browned.

"You want it, that's fine," her dad said.

That evening, Jessy and Twyla huddled over the floor in Jessy's room. Both their doors were open, and a record was playing loud enough in Twyla's to hear the music in both rooms, but not so loud that their parents would yell at them from downstairs.

Jessy picked the window-shade roll up and weighed it with her hand.

"It's kind of like a scroll," she said. "I bet you could roll it up so it would look like, maybe something Egyptian."

"It could pass for papyrus," Twyla agreed.

The paper unrolled from the top, and had a slightly ragged edge on the bottom, which was sealed up, laminated, but had cracked a little and unraveled. In the center of the bottom hung a circle, like a donut, covered closely with yarn.

Twyla pulled the paper down with the circle, and then she rolled it up again. She seemed to be testing it out. Then she pulled the paper down again. It made a satisfying rustling sound.

"I think it's haunted papyrus," Twyla said.

"Paper can't be haunted," Jessy scoffed.

"Who says?"

She took a pencil off Jessy's desk and started sketching a big picture on the surface of the shade. The bottom was the ground, and on it she drew a big house. A haunted house. In the upper story she made a triangular protrusion, and a window she covered with thin spider web. The other windows she drew in, and then added lines to show they were cracked or empty. And in one of them, a thin, unformed face.

"It's like the Addams Family house," Jessy said.

"Yup."

On the horizontal line representing the lawn, Twyla added a spindly, sickly tree, and Jessy put in a tombstone shaped like a cross, that was leaning slightly, like the Tower of Pisa. Then Twyla drew some crooked bats in the sky, and smoke coming out of the chimney that turned into a shape that might be a ghost. In the background, there was a curved road leading off in the distance, like the Yellow Brick Road, only Jessy colored it orange.

"It's too bad this needs some kind of rod," Twyla said. "Or we could make it a real shade you could put on your window."

26

That shade was the same shape, but the material was more plasticky. It wouldn't work to write on it, and her parents would kill her if she tried.

"But maybe you'll find something to do with it," Twyla added. Jessy didn't know what to say. It looked really cool, like the cover of a spooky book.

"Thanks," she said.

"Well, your fluorescent drawings really liven up the living room," Twyla said. "So I might as well help the cause."

****

Jessy's bedtime was a full half hour earlier than anyone she knew, which was completely unfair. Karma didn't even have a bedtime. Every night, after she went grudgingly to bed, Jessy sat awake, listening to the TV shows her parents were watching downstairs, and pictured what was going on, like it was on the radio.

At nine, her mom would come by to make sure her light was out, so she'd be under the covers, pretending to be asleep, in case anyone popped a head in. Her mom usually just lingered outside the door, and then went back downstairs. Her bedtime was annoying, but it gave her time to think about things. Sometimes she picked out an actor she liked, and made up long, drawn-out stories about their future life together. But this time of year she had the Halloween story to ponder.

In the dark, thinking of what might come through her own door, she tried to decide if she'd be more scared of something real, like a killer, who actually had a body. Or would it be worse if there was some kind of ghost monster, that could seep into her room from somewhere else? She imagined that being really silent, with padded feet.

Even if it was dead people, coming out of their graves, it seemed like it would be worse if you could see their bodies, if they were physical and could grab you. But then, they'd be something you could get away from. It would be freaky, and people would get hysterical, and stuff. But you could run home and lock your doors and call the police.

If they were spirits, though, you might not even know they were there. But they'd still be dead. They could sneak up behind you and

27

mess with your mind. If they could get out of the ground, they'd probably be able to go through walls, too. One could be in her room right now.

Eventually she listened to her parents come up the stairs and go to bed. She was still awake. Late that night, her bedroom door slowly creaked open, sounding just like a door from a scary movie.

"You awake?" a voice whispered. It was just Twyla, tiptoeing over to the bed. Jessy sat right up.

"What'd you do tonight?" she asked.

"There were two kegs down at the gravel pits."

"Who was there?"

"Everybody."

Twyla always said her class was cool because everyone partied together. Jessy could already tell her grade wasn't going to be like that, when they got into high school.

Tonight she told Jessy about seeing the Homecoming Queen fall on her face because she was so drunk, and how a girl from their church threw up in some guy's car. Then she said, "You're supposed to be asleep."

"I'm thinking," Jessy said.

"Well, if you're going to stay awake anyway, there's something you need. I'll be right back." Twyla crept out, silent, to her own room. She came back with her old transistor radio, a plastic string hanging out of it, connected to a small plastic earpiece.

"It's not as strong as the radio in the kitchen, but sometimes, late at night, you can get WLS in. If you keep it under the covers, they'll never know you have it."

She swatted Jessy slightly on the head, and said, "Don't let the bed bugs get ya."

Jessy wedged the lumpy plastic carefully into her ear, and then strained in the dark to read the numbers on the transistor's small read-out. She turned the plastic dial, which was round, with a sharp triangular edge. Twyla was right; eventually WLS started to come in, faintly, and she tweaked the dial, with the tiniest possible movements, until she got the best signal she could. She kept the sound turned down really low. It shouldn't matter with the earpiece, but it made her nervous to have it above a whisper.

WLS was officially the coolest radio station in the world. They played all the newest songs, and ran ads for movies that would never play at their theater, and they gave away free tickets for concerts. Rock bands came right to the same town as the listeners, which Jessy couldn't even imagine. The contests didn't help them any: she and Twyla pretended they might get to be the tenth caller, but the station was in Chicago, unimaginably far away. Even so, even when it was crackling or fading out, like it was doing now, it sounded as close as the country music station right in town.

****

At school, the word was out: Halloween costumes were in. Jessy and Karma made the trip right after school. The dime store looked like it had been there for a hundred years, dignified on the outside, with its big glass windows set into red brick. Inside it was a crazy jumble, full of aisles squeezed into spaces that were too narrow for them, and so much stuff crammed in that the light seemed to get lost in there and turn dim.

Among the rows and rows of tall shelves were a handful of areas that they regularly patrolled. The candy was on the shelf facing the counter, so the women who worked there in the red smocks could watch them carefully while they were deciding. Then there was the school supply aisle, which had been bursting with new stuff just a month or so ago, but had already whittled back to the standards: a handful of notebooks, pens, the things you might run out of during the year.

On the other side of the toys were the craft supplies. The far back of the store had a counter, surrounded by lower shelves and bolts of cloth, drawers full of threads and thimbles and flimsy envelopes with tissue-paper pattern books in them. Behind that, in the corner, was the pet shop. Against the wall, goldfish swam around in rectangular tanks, and a few small birds chirped, sounding annoyed. Years ago, there had been a monkey in a cage, but now the monkey was gone. He'd never been for sale, and kids argued about whether the monkey was really dead, or had just retired from the store.

Normally, Jessy's top priority was the couple of racks of record albums. Those were by the front window, across from the gumball machines and the mechanical horse, whose head she still sometimes patted on the star-shaped patch of white, remembering when she was really little, and loved to ride on his glossy brown back.

She kept a close eye on what had come in, even though she almost never had enough money for an album, despite saving since her birthday, when she'd gotten a whole five-dollar bill. That's why Twyla had gotten her job at the Freezy Stand, so she could buy records. Of course, that was only open in the summer, so now that school had started Twyla was home more often, and grumbling about how poor she was.

Today Jessy and Karma ignored the whole rest of the store, and went straight to the center, where a long clothing rack had been shoved in, full of hanging costumes. Some of them were cloth outfits, like thin, slippery capes, and some flannel shirts with bits of fake straw poking out of the wrists and neck. Most of them, though, were printed costumes, like elaborate plastic bags, with matching plastic masks hanging down where the necks would be.

Over in the first set of shelves, a display had been set up, masks dangling from it, and decorations printed on thin cardboard. Below that were some rows of makeup kits, and even some tubes to make fake scars and warts. Jessy didn't know anyone who'd ever used them, but the dime store had them every Halloween. Then there was a line of trick-or-treat buckets. Most of them were the round orange jack-o-lantern buckets, with their slightly indented black features, and then a couple of black cat heads.

Karma swished quickly through the hangers, pausing to inspect a few more closely.

"They look like pajamas," she said.

Jessy had always wanted to get one of the expensive costumes with a matching mask, just on principle, but she had to agree. The store-bought ones were fancier, but up close, you could tell how flimsy they were. The vampire capes didn't even look like they were made out of real material, and the ghost was just a long white shirt that wouldn't fool anybody, especially not with the goofy, cartoon-like expression on the mask.

They looked over the cardboard decorations. One was a skull with a large furry spider crawling out of its eye socket, and a half-burnt candle next to it. Jessy's mom would never let her hang that one up. There were some corn shocks and familiar-looking ghosts, nothing too special. Then Jessy spotted two decorations with a similar style, like overgrown illustrations from the same book. One was a cute little witch, riding a broom, black cape flaring, with a yellow full moon behind her, and the other was a big orange jack-o-lantern, with a fluffy black kitten sitting inside of it. They reminded her of the characters from her own Halloween stories.

Jessy had brought enough money with her, and she'd still have a little left over for later in the season. So she had to buy them before they were gone.

Before they left, they inspected the penny candy. It wasn't really a penny anymore, but there was still an assortment of small things you could buy for a nickel, and up to a dime, you had more choices.

Karma bought some candy bottle caps.

"What flavor are you getting?" Jessy asked.

"Root beer."

Jessy made a face.

"The root beer ones are gross."

"The orange are gross."

"You're crazy," Jessy said.

They left by the back door, into the alleyway, which was filled with beat-up garbage cans, and cars wedged into small spaces. They walked down the block, behind the movie theater, until the alley crossed the sidewalk, right next to where the movie theater's side door opened. There were stories about kids, maybe Twyla's age, sneaking in through the door, but it wasn't very hidden. It was sitting right there on the sidewalk. As Twyla always said, it was hard to get away with anything around there.

They walked back to Jessy's house, Karma wriggling open the bottle caps package, Jessy swinging the thin bag.

****

"The costumes are in at the dime store," Jessy announced at dinner. She had already taped both of her new decorations to the outside of her bedroom door.

"So, what are you going to be this year?" her Dad asked, dishing up his chili.

"I haven't decided yet," she said.

"Well, you're not buying any plastic masks," her Mom said.

Jessy didn't even think she wanted one, but that still made her mad. She knew some kids who got a new plastic mask every year.

"That's not fair. I've never had one."

"It's just a waste of money, and you wouldn't like it," her Mom went on. "They smell funny, and they're uncomfortable, and you'd just keep taking it off."

"I wouldn't take it off."

"And the string will break." Her mom turned to Twyla and said, "Remember that ghost costume? We finally agreed to get you the plastic mask?"

"It's not my fault the string broke." Twyla rolled her eyes.

"You hadn't even left the house yet. We rigged up the string, and how long did it stay on your head?"

It had all been ruined for Jessy before she was even old enough to remember. "Thanks a lot," she mumbled.

"You don't want one of those masks anyway," Twyla said. "Those are for kids with no imagination."

"That's certainly not your problem," their mom said.

****

The best day of the week, at least at school, was when they went to the library. Jessy and Karma had a vendetta against the old librarian, who always kept them from checking out books because they weren't in the right grade for them. She looked over their selections and decided if they were too advanced. But she didn't even know them, so she really had no idea what they could read.

On one visit, after having some of her books rejected, Jessy tried to check out a book she'd really liked when she was little, full of pictures of kittens, and when that had been rejected as too young for her, she almost got into trouble for being sarcastic. After that, she mainly checked out adult novels from the public library, where they never cared how old she was.

Now they had a new school librarian, who was young and blonde and wore shortish skirts. They saw her at the Freezy Stand with her husband, acting like real people. She didn't seem like a teacher at all. And she loved that Jessy and Karma liked to read, so she encouraged them to check out whatever they wanted.

Everyone was supposed to get a book on a science subject, for a report, and apart from that, they could check out something for themselves. Karma wandered purposefully up and down the fiction aisle, trying to find a book she hadn't read yet about girls in boarding school.

Ever since they had read *The Secret Language* a couple of years ago, Karma had been addicted to boarding school books. Jessy suspected that deep down, she hoped she'd get sent to boarding school someday. Not that any of them had ever heard of a boarding school in any of the towns around there.

Jessy had read a few of Karma's books, and they were okay, but she didn't think she'd like boarding school itself. The stories were always full of girls rebelling against the rules, and it seemed to her that they had more than enough rules in public school. Besides, Karma's parents were great, much mellower than Jessy's, so she didn't know why she'd want to go somewhere you could never get away from the teachers. Just the idea of the teachers she knew telling her when to go to bed … Yikes. Life was hard enough.

In the science section, one of her classmates, Kim, was scanning the shelves, looking for inspiration.

"What's your subject going to be?" she asked.

"Astronomy," Jessy said without hesitating. That was her favorite part of science. She had a folder covered in pictures of constellations on the front, from this year's school supplies.

"I wouldn't do a report on astronomy," Kim said. "It's bad."

"What's wrong with it?" Jessy was puzzled.

"It's a kind of fortune telling," she answered.

"Do you mean astrology?" Jessy asked. "Like your horoscope?"

"It's the same thing," Kim said.

Bad or not, Jessy grabbed a book about the Milky Way, and then continued wandering around the nonfiction, waiting for something to jump out at her. And it did. The hand of fate was always at work in the library.

She spotted a matching series of tall, slim books with glossy black spines. They were like encyclopedias, but the volumes were full of pictures, so they were shaped differently. There were a bunch of sets like this on different subjects, but she had never noticed this one before. She slid the one called *Magic, Numbers and Symbols* away from its spot, and opened it right up to two pages about palmistry. There was a big line drawing of a hand, covered with tiny arrows and numbers and words, like an elaborate miniature map. The traditional Halloween potential of fortune telling clearly made it the right book for the Free Reading period of Reading.

****

After school, they hung out with Troy and Scott and Corey. They sat hanging listlessly on the merry-go-round, not trying to push it, although it wobbled slightly on its axis, turning them occasionally, very slowly. Karma hung her legs down over the side, scuffing the sand with her feet. All around the merry-go-round ran a circle of foot track.

Jessy sat further back, tucked inside the bars like she was on the tilt-o-wheel, or trying to steer it with the forked metal. Troy stood up in the middle, and every once in a while he would push his weight to one side, trying to turn them faster, but Karma's feet kept slowing them down again.

"We need to go to the cemetery sometime," Jessy said. "I need to do some research."

"Research for what?" Corey asked.

"Jessy writes a Halloween story every year," Karma said. Jessy wished she wouldn't say anything about that; it kind of embarrassed her.

"It's nothing," she said.

"Like a spooky story?" Troy asked.

Jessy shrugged.

"That story you wrote in Reading last year was really good," he said. "About the horse."

"I wouldn't go to the cemetery," Corey said.

Their gazes all turned in its direction. They could see it from there, in the distance, over the low hollow of the football field. All those dead people, waiting quietly for them.

"Why not?" Jessy said. "I go there all the time." She and Karma had made up plenty of stories about the people whose old, faded names were chiseled into the grey, mossy stones.

"Because." She sounded stubborn, like it was totally self-evident that nobody would want to go there. "Because it's the cemetery."

They just kind of looked at her.

"People are buried there."

"Sure," Troy said. "If they weren't, they'd just be all over the place."

"Oh, gross," Corey said. Then, "You shouldn't go anywhere where people are buried. It's just ... you don't know what'll happen if you do."

34

"You know," Troy said. "My big brother and some of his friends snuck in there one night to drink beer, and something really weird happened to them."

"Like what?" Jessy asked.

"Well, they found a place deep inside the cemetery, where they thought nobody could see them from the road. There were some trees sheltering them. And they were hanging out, just BS-ing, you know, having a few beers, talking about football." Troy's brother was a big deal on the football team. "Then suddenly, one of them noticed that there was a blue light in the cemetery with them, a little bit away. And they could see it sort of -- floating toward them."

"Get out of here," Karma said.

"Seriously. So one of the guys says, it's the cops. And they all start running. But it wasn't on the road." The cemetery was crisscrossed with paved pathways, wide enough for a single car. "So it can't be a cop car, or it would be running into the tombstones. And my brother realized that it was floating above the ground. He said he was running, and he stopped, because it was coming right at him. And it came closer to him, and then it just disappeared."

"It did not," Jessy said.

"I'm not making it up. He was really freaked out. They think it was a UFO."

Scott immediately perked up. There was a book on Project Blue Book at the library, and over the summer, Jessy and Karma had made UFO watching notebooks, with pages ready to record their findings, if they ever saw a UFO. One night they'd gone over and sat around in Scott's backyard, watching for UFOs, and he'd copied their format to make his own notebook. He'd already asked for a telescope for Christmas.

"It could have been a UFO," he said. "But that's totally different from a ghost."

"The highway is right on the other side of the cemetery," Karma said. "It could have been headlights, reflecting on something."

"And if they were drinking beer," Jessy said. "Maybe they didn't -- I don't know -- have their wits about them."

"I've seen him drunk a million times," Troy said. He pushed his weight as a little brush of wind started them moving slowly. "I'm sure they saw something."

"See," Corey said. "That's exactly why."

"It wasn't anything to do with dead people," Karma said, reasonably.

"No, but something strange can happen when you go in there."

"Lots of people go to cemeteries, and it's perfectly normal," Karma went on. "There's someone who mows the grass. And what about when there's a funeral?"

"If you're going to a funeral, or when you're going to put flowers on a grave, that's one thing. But you have to have a reason."

That made sense to everybody.

But how would the spirits, or whoever, know whether you had a reason or not?

"Maybe they saw a will-o-the-wisp," Jessy suggested.

"A what?"

"I've read about them. They're mysterious lights that appear in the swamp. Some people think it's some kind of gas that causes the lights, but some people think it's like a tricky ghost."

"Tricky?"

"They flicker in the night, like a candle. And if people are lost, they sometimes follow the light, and when they do, they get lured deeper in the swamp, and then they drown."

"That's just like, fireflies or something," Scott said.

"Maybe the ghost wants company," Karma said.

"If you're going to the cemetery, I'm not going to play with you this weekend," Corey said.

When the other kids left, Jessy and Karma teeter-tottered for a while. They had a few normal up and downs, and then, when her seat hit the ground, Jessy settled all her weight down and planted her feet on the sand, freezing the motion.

"Farmer, farmer, let me down," Karma said.

"What will you give me if I let you down?"

"I'll give you … a new bike."

Jessy thought about it for a minute.

"A ten-speed. With a basket," Karma elaborated.

Jessy lifted her weight. They had a few more seesaws, and then Karma trapped her up in the air, her feet dangling at her sides.

"Farmer, farmer, let me down."

"What will you give me if I let you down?"

"I'll give you … a pony."

"A pony?" Karma scoffed.

"A horse," Jessy went on. Karma appeared to ponder deeply on the subject. Jessy kept going, "An Arabian stallion, just like the one in *King of the Wind*. With a jet black mane and tail."

"Okay, deal."

They could go on like this all day. A movie theater, stocked with all the new movies. and someone to make popcorn all day, for Jessy. A professional basketball court for Karma. All the candy they could eat. When it started to get late, usually someone would end up with "all the money in the world." Nobody could top that, and that was the end of the game.

They started on a route back from the playground.

"We'll go past the Murder House," Jessy said.

"I'm not scared."

"I know you're not scared."

The house was across the street, the way they were walking, and set in, so it seemed a little out of the way.

There were a lot of bushes and trees around, brambling all over it. One large clump of pine trees near the sidewalk was almost as tall as the house, with giant branches that fanned down to make a secluded spot underneath. Kids didn't go too close to the house, but they did sneak under the branches to drink beer and peppermint schnapps. Younger kids scooted under them, too, collecting the empty bottles and swishing them around, to see if there was anything worth trying to drink.

On the other side of the house, there were lilac bushes next to the sidewalk, and in the spring, when Jessy and Karma tore off bunches of blossoms, Twyla called them ghost lilacs, and said they were going to be haunted by their spirits.

"Flowers don't have ghosts," Karma would insist.

"How do you know?" Twyla would ask. "They're living things, just like you and me."

They looked up at the house, standing so majestic and set-apart, on that huge lawn, with the long walk-way leading up to the door.

"We're definitely going to ring the doorbell this year," Jessy said.

"That's what we said last year."

"We just didn't get around to it."

They knew that nobody lived there, but that didn't matter. It was trick or treating.

Over the years, they'd had some intense discussions on the subject. Some older houses had metal plaques by the doorbells that said "No Peddlers," engraved in old-fashioned-looking letters. Jessy had thought peddlers were characters out of fairy tales and picture books, but Twyla told her it was just a way to say you shouldn't come to their door selling anything.

"It's like No Soliciting," Twyla said, which they also saw on a few doors.

That was another intriguingly big word, just to say "Don't ask us for money."

But was trick or treating the same as soliciting? When they came across one of the signs, Karma thought they shouldn't try it, because the people who lived there were going to be grumpy, and not give them candy.

"My mom always says there are some old people who don't believe in trick or treating. They think it's the same as begging, and they'll get mad."

That was like the cranky people who were always so worried about their lawns.

"So they get mad," Twyla said. "What are they going to do?"

"I don't know. Maybe they'll call the police."

"It's not against the law to trick or treat."

"Maybe they'll say that we're trespassing. We're in their yard, on their steps."

Their parents had threatened them about trespassing the time they caught Jessy and Karma playing in an empty house. The doors had been taken off, so nothing but plastic sheets covered the empty spaces, to keep rain out, and those hadn't even been tied down.

There wasn't anything inside they could hurt themselves with; they'd just run around in the empty rooms. But their parents agreed that they could get in trouble for something like that, because it was trespassing.

Of course, they ran around all the time, playing in other people's yards, and their garages, and never thought anything of it. Sometimes it was hard to predict what was going to get you in trouble.

"It's Halloween," Twyla said. "That's when you get to try things. You get to go places and do things you don't normally get to do."

With the Murder House, though, Jessy was secretly afraid that, after all this time, all that emptiness, no sign of life at all, the door might suddenly open. What would happen then?

Well, they'd scream and run.

There were worse things than screaming and running.

But what if a hand reached out from the creaking door, and they were frozen in place, and skeletal fingers grabbed at them, and dragged them inside?

****

During Free Reading that week, Jessy read her magic book, about how forms of magic were practiced in civilizations since the beginning of time. There was divination (the palms and the runes), there was healing magic, and there was Black Magic. The book capitalized it that way: Black Magic, for when you wanted to do some harm. It had color photos of voodoo rag dolls, with stick pins poking out of their cloth heads, and woodcut-style drawings of old women on broomsticks. Jessy immediately started thinking about some new fluorescent drawings: a cauldron, flames spilling up from underneath it, with a ladle sticking out, and maybe a dangling frog. Not that it would look like a frog.

"Double, Double, Toil and Trouble," the headline read, which made it sound like Black Magic was something you really had to work hard at. Like geometry.

Of course she'd heard of Black Magic before, everybody had, but the section on Ceremonial Magic was new to her. It talked about using symbolism, so that one thing would represent another, like a pumpkin could represent Halloween. Or like when *MAD* magazine used the dollar sign, and the other weird marks from the typewriter, for the swear words.

Then there was another big section with charts of "correspondences," sets of things standing for each other. The book said you could take small fabric bags and fill them with objects, matching the color of the bag to what you put in it, so they all represented the same thing. And there was a whole sidebar about "seals." Those were illustrations of circles, and in each circle there were different shapes, and each one was supposed to mean something.

So for love, you'd use the color red for the bag, and the number would be two, and you'd put in a rose head, and then there was a specific seal with squiggles that stood for love. Then you could use the whole bag as a kind of talisman.

Jessy was surprised at how practical this all seemed. It wasn't like waving your hands in the air and thinking "poof," I can make whatever I want to happen. You could follow the charts and then, who knows? Maybe it would work. She just had to decide what she wanted.

The color she was drawn to, looking at the picture of richly colored bags in a silky-looking jumble, was purple. Purple stood for wisdom. Its number was seven. Its flower was the lily. And the seal was the Seal of Solomon. From Sunday School, she knew all about the pretending to cut the baby in half, but there was also the Song of Songs, which she read in the pew on several Sundays, waiting for church to start. Even the Bible had good parts.

She could make a paper seal easily enough. They'd made coins out of yellow construction paper before, and that was close enough. And then what would she do with the bag? The book said you could keep it, or that sometimes people threw them into running water, or buried them. It seemed obvious to her that Halloween would be the best possible time to do some magic, so she could always bury it on Halloween.

She couldn't wait to tell Karma.

Even while she was thinking about it, she didn't know if she really believed in magic, any more than if she really believed in ghosts. Deep down, she believed that she was as capable of understanding things as she would ever be, but she didn't have a lot of information.

If she actually saw a ghost, then she'd pretty much have to believe in them. Just like with UFOs. She thought it would be really cool to see a UFO, but she didn't believe Troy's brother had seen one. Twyla had told her too many stories about him. Twyla thought most of the football players were idiots, and she had facts to back her up. Even so, there was Project Blue Book, after all, and people kept writing books about mysterious things they had seen. So you just never knew.

That was an idea for a story, popped right into her mind! She turned to the pages in the back of her notebook, and jotted down, "Think they see a UFO. Really a ghost." Or maybe it went the other way, where they thought they saw a ghost, but it was really a UFO. But that would be science fiction, and that seemed a lot more difficult.

****

Everyone went to the football game that night. They split off from their families and gathered in a group, Corey sitting with Jessy and Karma, in the top row of bleachers, which weren't actually high up, since they were all carved into a curved hill around the football field. They screamed until they were halfway hoarse, and in between caring about the game, they yelled greetings, and poked at the friends sitting in front of them. At half-time, as they all milled around the Concession Stand, Scott and Troy came up to them, looking around like they were afraid of being watched.

"We were talking about those lights in the cemetery," he said. "Do you guys want to check it out? See if there's anything to it."

They turned and looked at the visible dark area where the cemetery was, hardly more than a block away.

"Yes!" Jessy said.

"Right now?" Karma asked.

"We could sneak over while the game is going on," Jessy suggested. "But there are probably too many people around."

"Yeah," Scott said. "We wouldn't want anyone to know." Everyone knew you weren't supposed to go in the cemetery after dark, even if they didn't believe in ghosts.

"And besides, we want to see the rest of the game," Karma said.

"We'll all be going out on Halloween," Scott said.

"If there's any time ghosts are going to be out, it'll be Halloween, right?" Jessy asked.

"That makes sense," Karma agreed. "So we can find out once and for all."

"But, we still want to get candy," Troy said.

Everyone agreed to that.

"So we can meet up after trick or treating, and walk over to the cemetery."

The crowds were wandering back to the stands, so the game was going to be starting soon.

Corey had been quiet during the discussion, but as they neared their old seats she asked, "You're really going to do it?"

"Sure, why not?"

"But you're not really going to ring the doorbell at the Murder House."

"Well, I'm not scared to ring the doorbell," Jessy said, more determined than ever not to wimp out this year.

They won the game, and afterwards, Jessy's parents hunted her down.

"We want to stay for the bonfire," she said.

"There's not going to be a bonfire," her Dad said. "It's too windy."

****

Saturday afternoon, Jessy sat in her room, stretched out on the bed. She had just started a new book from the Scholastic Book Club, called *Spooks and Spirits and Shadowy Shapes*. She was deeply enthralled in a story about some kids out trick or treating, who were walking around the block and creeping themselves out. That made total sense, since it seemed just like her own neighborhood, and she could imagine perfectly how creepy that might be, under the right circumstances. There was a knock on the door, and Twyla stuck her head in without getting an answer.

"Are you home?" she asked.

"Yeah."

Twyla came in and closed the door behind her. Then she noticed that the haunted papyrus was hanging in the window, rigged up and bulging a little awkwardly over the top of the real shade.

"Nice," she said, then added, "I have something for you."

"What?"

There was a small book in her hand.

"I've been going through some of those papers in that box, you know, the one with the window shade? It came from the Storvigs. Joe says it was a bunch of stuff that came from their mom's family, that they decided to get rid of. Did you ever hear the story about Mrs. Peterson?"

"No," Jessy said, like it was Twyla who was stupid.

"Well, Joe says Mrs. Peterson was his grandma's sister, who became kind of a recluse. She was a widow, and she lived by herself near the end of town. His grandma said that she always thought she was cursed, even before her husband died, since she was a teenager."

"Cursed how?" Jessy asked.

"That she was doomed to unhappiness, and anyone she loved would die a horrible death. When her husband proposed, she kept refusing. She finally gave in, but then when he died, she got kind of -- crazy."

"What happened to her?" Jessy asked.

"I don't know for sure. She died, probably just old age. Joe's grandma died a while back, that's why they had those boxes of stuff that belonged to her, and the old furniture to get rid of. They finally got around to it now."

They both sat for another minute. Curses didn't really exist, Jessy thought. Just like ghosts didn't. They were just stories.

"So anyway, I found this in the box." Twyla handed over a small, old-looking book. It was slightly stiff, like a hardcover, but it had a paper cover, almost like a magazine. Jessy could tell right away that it was old, just from the style of it, and the way the paper edge looked slightly discolored.

On the cover was a painting of an enormous orange moon, a startled look on its face, peering down at a scene where a green-faced witch stood in front of a gnarled tree. Wispy shapes of narrow ghosts, with tiny faces, stared out of the night sky background.

"*The Orange and Black Book*," it said. "*Suggestions for Hallowe'en*."

"Wow," Jessy breathed.

She opened the front cover delicately, as if she was afraid it would crumble in her hands. But once she touched the creamy paper, she could feel how sturdy it was. The print was fairly small, and the pages were full of fine line drawings, girls with slick bobbed hair in knee-length gowns, printed in Harlequin patterns, with tutu-like protruding skirts, all inked in orange and black. The whole book was in orange and black and white.

"It's like a catalog," Twyla said. "You could order the patterns for the dresses, and all these paper decorations from it, for Halloween parties."

"When is this from?" Jessy asked, turning it around, looking at the front and back covers. There it was. 1925. That was a long time ago.

"Wow," she said again.

"I don't think Dad'll care that I gave this to you," Twyla said. "But I don't know if you want to mention it."

"Probably not," Jessy said. That was always the safest course of action.

After dinner, she stayed up in her room with the book. The first section was titled "How to Throw a Hobgoblin Party," and she imagined herself hobgoblining like crazy. A two-page spread showed an enormous hall, like the old high school gym, only with giant orange chandeliers, dripping with black crepe paper banners. A long table was spread with a solid, bright orange tablecloth, and on it, a punchbowl sat on top of a lacy, spiderwebbed doily. The inside of the punchbowl was orange, too, with daintily drawn orange slices floating in it.

The women were all slim and delicate, wearing burglar masks with black cat ears, or half-masks with small pointed devil horns.

Another part of the book was about a "Homey Harvest Home," which was a party to have in the house, for friends. The Hobgoblin Party was for a "club," although it didn't specify what kind of club they were talking about. They advised you to use every room in the house for the Harvest Home Party. "Don't forget the attic, or the coal scuttle."

Paper ghosts and paper pumpkins dangled everywhere; paper skeletons sat on top of hay bales; and ruffled paper centerpieces folded out into fat, serious-faced owls.

The book also described a bunch of different fortune-telling games, which they already said were old-fashioned. "At Hallowe'en, the veil between the worlds is at its thinnest, and in some cases, it can even be parted," or at least that's what you were supposed to tell your guests.

If her mom found about the book, she'd want to put it in the Jack-o-Lantern Box. Jessy had a section in her bookcase that made up her Halloween library, so before bed, she tucked it in safely with those books.

Besides *Spooks and Spirits and Shadowy Shapes*, she also had one called *Witches, Pumpkins, and Grinning Ghosts*. She still had the *Georgie* book, about a little ghost, and *Georgie's Halloween*, even though they were for little kids, because the drawings were so beautiful. They were all black and white and orange, too, just like the *Orange and Black Book*. Next to those was *Something Wicked This Way Comes*, a grown-up looking paperback with a shiny white spine.

On the same shelf was a random assortment of Trixie Beldens and Cherry Ameses, passed down from Twyla, along with a book called *The Silver Spoon Mystery*. It seemed like there was nothing that couldn't be haunted, everywhere had a mystery, it was continually *The Mystery of the Haunted This and That*.

The Mystery at the Monkey Bars, she thought.

The Mystery of the Haunted Record Player.

The Phantom at the Dime Store.

That last one almost sounded like the title of a real book.

To Trixie Belden or Cherry Ames, a story like the one about the lights in the cemetery would just be another mystery. But if she wrote about it, then she'd have to know how the mystery was solved, and what it really meant. It wasn't like real life, where they could go out on Halloween night to be detectives, and just see what happened.

****

That night, Jessy went down to half-watch TV on the couch. Cupcake was sitting in the middle of the room, eyes closed, but her posture alert-looking. It was the Sphinx Pose. Twyla walked through, her jean jacket on, carrying the purse she'd made herself out of the butt of a pair of jeans, sewn together on the bottom where her legs used to stick out. She'd put patches on the back pockets, a heart with the American flag pattern inside it. Jessy had begged her sister to make one for her, but she didn't have any jeans to cut up.

Twyla had feathered her hair a little bit, a clip on one side with a real brown feather dangling from it, and she wore a pair of boots with really high heels, but not quite as high as platforms. Jessy had never seen them before. They made a clopping noise when Twyla went into the kitchen, and it caught everybody's attention.

Her mom got up from the corner chair where she was reading and followed Twyla into the kitchen.

"Where did you get those?" she demanded.

"I bought them."

"With what? You're always complaining about how poor you are right now."

"I saved my money. And it's none of your business."

"Don't take that tone with me," her mom snapped. "This isn't the first time I've noticed you wearing something you couldn't afford."

"Where do you think I got it from then?"

"I think it would be better if you told me."

"There's nothing to tell."

Jessy heard water running in the sink.

"Don't think you're going out tonight," their mom said.

"What?"

"I'm your mother. You go out when you have permission."

Twyla swore.

"That's it, young lady. You go right upstairs and take those clothes off. I don't know what you're trying to look like."

"I'm trying to look like me," Twyla cried. "And I'm going out."

"No, you're not."

"I have plans," she said. "You can't just tell me what to do at the last minute."

"I think your friends will get by without you at the bowling alley if you don't show up," Mom said, not even trying to disguise her sarcasm.

"I have plans and I'm keeping them, and you can't stop me," Twyla said. She stormed out of the house and slammed the door. Their mom marched into the living room.

"Where is your father?" she demanded.

Jessy felt frozen in place on the sofa. Cupcake had already run upstairs, and she wanted to follow, but at the same time she felt like she had to hold her ground.

"I guess he's in the workshop," she said, pretending to have been interrupted from her book, like she hadn't heard anything.

"Typical," her mom hissed, and headed in that direction.

****

After Sunday school the next morning, they went over to play at Karma's. Both of them had big houses with big yards, but Karma's was bigger, with an enormous yard, so when people saw it for the first time -- adults -- they always said something about having to mow the lawn. The house was shaped kind of like a barn, which seemed appropriate, since it was on the edge of town, with fields just past it.

Jessy especially loved its big porch, all enclosed, that had windows all the way around it. It was filled with dusty wicker furniture, and wooden shelves full of mismatched clay pots separated from their round clay bottoms, and half-empty bags of potting soil. An old stove from the old farmhouse sat on the porch, too, and they hid things in it.

Karma had two older brothers who had already left school, but her mom and dad didn't seem old enough. Her mom still looked young and pretty, even though her brown hair was getting to look a little grey around the edges. It was especially noticeable when she pulled it back in a pony tail, and all the scattered grey bits got bunched together. She still looked younger than Jessy's mom.

They ate summer sausage sandwiches up in Karma's room, which was painted light pink, with curtains of darker pink and seafoam green. She had a green thumb just like her mom, and in front of every window there were potfulls of African violets.

Jessy hauled the *Orange and Black Book* out of her bag, and handed it to Karma, who leafed through it while she told her the whole story.

"I want to be this one," Karma announced, pointing to a beautiful illustrated woman, wearing a long string of dangling orange beads, and holding a feathery black mask, something between an elegant owl and a glamorous bat, on a stick in front of her face.

"Maybe we could make masks on sticks," Jessy said. She had seen people carrying them at masquerade parties on TV shows.

They talked about that for a while, but suddenly Karma realized they'd have to hold the mask up the whole time, which would be tiring, and besides, it would be hard to trick or treat one-handed.

"I've always wondered," Jessy said. "Is Hallowe'en spelled like that pronounced the same way as plain old Halloween?"

"I think so," Karma said. "But then, it's hard to tell sometimes. Maybe it's more – Halloweeeeeen."

Before too long, Karma's mom asked if they wanted to help her dad with the pumpkins. He'd driven his truck in from her grandparents' old farm, just a little further out in the country, and he'd come back with the first of the season. One by one, arms full with the heavy curves, they carried the pumpkins from the truck into the garage. A lot of them had dirt lodged in their creases, and some leaked pale yellowish-green sap. The stems were ragged, where her dad had sawed the gnarly green stems off the vines with a big knife, and they were prickly, too. You could cut yourself on the stems if you weren't careful.

He'd already set up a couple of card tables on the cement floor of the garage, leaving the car parked outside in the driveway. They filled up with pumpkins, all different shades, some of them darker orange, some brighter, with rounded shapes and oddly flattened ones, and a few that were more vertical, with lumpy, almost gourd-like silhouettes.

A few squash were mixed in, too, looking like interesting aliens. Some were a waxy, sickly pink, and others were a dark, forest green, with warty skin and exposed curves shaped like big acorn tops. Jessy hated the squash on principle, just because of the way they tasted.

"This is just the beginning," Karma's dad said, carrying tomatoes in a big wooden basket, the slats dark with old water stains. "You girls are going to have a lot of jack-o-lanterns to choose from this year."

Jessy and Karma walked around, circling the pumpkins, looking them over, like they were judges at a professional pumpkin contest. Tables full of future jack-o-lanterns, waiting for the slaughter. They were already picking out which ones they wanted. Farmers in magazines were always competing to grow the biggest pumpkin, but the shape was much more important. Sometimes the bigger pumpkins were too lopsided, like they couldn't hold up their own weight. Besides, they'd be a pain to carve.

Character was maybe even more important. Rounder pumpkins made good faces, but so did the tall, thinner, more oblong ones. You always needed a variety: a snaggle-toothed goofy face, a cheerful pumpkin, one that looked especially sinister.

Jessy always wanted at least one jack-o-lantern with a classic batwing mouth, which seemed to go with triangular eyes. But she also had a fondness for the softer, moon-faced pumpkin, with rounded eyes, and even a rounded O for a mouth. Getting the scowly ones just right was a little harder, but when they turned out, they were probably the best.

Jessy walked home for dinner. She was wearing her jacket, so she wouldn't get nagged, and now that the sun was getting a little lower, she was glad she did. A faint smoky fume in the air told her that some people already had their wood stoves on.

When she got home, she pulled off her shoes, using one toe to pry the heel away from the heel of her foot. Then she threw her book bag down inside the door. Her mom was right there.

"You need to start wearing a better jacket," she said.

"I was fine," Jessy said, taking off her jacket and hanging it up in the alcove.

"Dinner's almost ready."

Cupcake was lying on the floor in the living room, stretched out on her side, looking like a big pillow, with her fluffiest part sticking up. Jessy sat down on the ground and pressed the side of her face against the cat's side. She could feel the gentle pressure of the breathing, up and down, and stuck her nose into the fluffy patch. The cat stretched, both front paws and back paws hooking into lazy crooked extensions, like she was too sleepy to keep them straight. It was like she was curling around an invisible ball.

Jessy could hear her dad coming up the stairs from the basement. The whole house creaked when anyone was on those steps.

"She hasn't come home yet," she heard her mom say, voice low and kind of urgent. "And she hasn't called."

"Did you call her friend?"

"Yes. Her mother hasn't seen her. If you can trust anything they say, these kids she's been hanging out with lately."

Jessy sat up to listen, continuing to stroke Cupcake slowly, scritching her under the chin. Half-awake, the cat tilted her chin up higher, purring.

They had an uncomfortable dinner, and Jessy forced herself to eat the cream corn. She tried to hold her breath while she was swallowing, but that didn't make it taste any better. Thinking about Twyla made her feel anxious. She'd seen plenty of TV shows about teenage runaways, and they never ended well.

Of course, those kids were always running away in New York or Los Angeles, where there was a lot more trouble for them to get into. Here, she didn't know where somebody would even go. Unless she ran away to New York or L.A., which would take a long time.

About seven o'clock, suddenly the front door swung open, and Twyla walked in, wearing the same clothes as yesterday, like nothing was wrong.

"Hey," she said.

Their mom was on her feet in a second.

"Where have you been?" she demanded.

"There was an extra youth group meeting," Twyla said. "It's on the calendar."

"You're grounded for a month," their mom said. "Two months. Maybe until you graduate."

"Give me a break," Twyla said.

"I mean it."

"Maybe I won't graduate at all. What'll you do then?"

"I want you to go upstairs right now and go to your room."

Twyla swung her purse over her shoulder.

"That's just where I want to go."

She breezed by, looking totally unconcerned.

Later on, Jessy was in the kitchen, drinking a cup of cocoa a spoonful at a time, with the big radio on. She could hear her mom and Twyla talking in the living room.

"Can I have some toast?" Twyla was saying. "Bread and water?"

"Do whatever you want," her mom said, sounding defeated. "You always do anyway."

"I wish."

"Don't take that tone with me. I mean what I said about being grounded."

"I agree. I'm grounded. I just don't want to talk about it."

"And I need you to be responsible for once in your life. I need you to come home right after school tomorrow. I'm going to a sale with your father, and I don't know when we'll get back. But I'm assuming it's going to be fairly late. It's a long drive. If I can't trust you to do this one thing for me ..." she trailed off.

"I'll come home right after school."

"Someone has to be here when Jessy gets home, so I'm serious about this."

"Mom," Twyla's voice sounded less argumentative, but Jessy's attention had gotten perked. "She's not a baby."

"I know she's not a baby. I even know you're not a baby."

"I'll come right home, I promise. But she could take care of herself."

"I know she can. But she doesn't have to. You're going to make dinner, and you're both going to stay out of trouble for one night."

"Don't worry. I'll be straight home, Jessy will come straight home, we won't get into any trouble. Everything will be fine."

"Okay," their mom said. "You can make a pizza."

Great! Jessy thought in the other room.

"But that doesn't mean you're off the hook. You're still in trouble. I'm not forgetting anything."

"Fine." Twyla sounded generous in defeat. Magnanimouse. "Oh, and does this mean I'm grounded from Yearbook?" She hadn't wanted to sign up for that, but their mom had insisted.

"Go have your toast."

Jessy leaned back in the chair, fiddling nonchalant with the radio dial, pretending the reception had been a little funky.

"You come home right after school tomorrow," Twyla said, knowing she'd heard the whole thing. "Or else. No Karma, no library."

****

"There's a movie on I want to watch tonight," Jessy said. She was glad she'd put off negotiating with her mom about TV rights. There was no point getting into it with her if Twyla was going to be in charge.

"Anything good?" Twyla opened the fridge and stared into it, completely uninterested in either Jessy or its contents.

"It's a vampire movie."

"Oh, no." She stood up, straightened, her face stern and disapproving. She looked exactly like their mom.

"It's an old movie. Black and white."

Their TV was black and white, but they both knew what she meant.

"I won't get scared, I promise."

"The whole point of a movie like that is to get scared," Twyla said. "You better not get scared and then not be able to sleep. I'm in enough trouble."

"I won't get scared," Jessy insisted. Twyla just stared at her, and her resolve started to wilt.

"I promise, if I do get scared, if I can't sleep, I won't tell Mom and Dad. Cross my heart."

"Okay then."

A lot of times, around Halloween, one of the local stations would play a spooky movie every day after school. Then when it got to be November, the show would disappear again. Jessy and Twyla would watch the movies, and then Jessy had nightmares. One year, she watched a movie called *The Blob* all by herself, and it was the scariest thing she'd ever seen. She had a terrible fear that something was going to just … absorb her.

Ever since then, her mom tried to forbid her from watching scary movies, but that just made her want to watch them even more.

Twyla got out the box of pizza mix. She made Jessy help with the crust, which was always the hardest job. They poured flour from the wax packet into a metal mixing bowl, and put in the water. At first it was pasty, then it got gluey, and eventually started to harden, about the time Jessy's wrist hurt from stirring. Twyla scraped it out of the bowl with a wooden spoon and plopped it down onto a rectangular cookie sheet. She smoothed it out, trying to make the dough even. There were always spots where the dough almost wore thin, and you could see the metal underneath it, but that was better than biting into clumps where it was too soft, when it was done.

Then Twyla opened the can of tomato sauce that came in the box. She poured it onto the center of the sheet, and let Jessy smooth that out with the back of a spoon until the dough was covered. There was a little plastic packet of oregano, too, that they scattered on top like it was glittery confetti, and then the packet of shredded cheese.

"I wish we could eat pizza every day," Jessy said.

"Maybe we'd get sick of it," Twyla said. But they agreed that didn't seem very likely.

Jessy wiped the fine floury residue onto her pant legs.

"Mom's really mad at you," she said, while Twyla was putting the pizza in the oven.

"She can't just do things like that at the last minute," Twyla said, stubborn. "I have my own life."

"I know."

Jessy tore open a little package of wet cat food for Cupcake, who'd been hanging around their feet. It seemed like she deserved a treat too.

"I had to go out," Twyla said. "I had a guitar lesson. And he already thinks I'm not taking it seriously, just because I'm a girl."

She had the scowl she gave when someone went into her room, just before she socked them.

"What about being a girl?"

"He says that Suzi Quatro proves that even when girls can play technically well, they just can't rock. And I said, even if that were true, which I don't know, does Barry Manilow prove that guys can't rock? We got in a big fight about it, but he's still giving me the lessons. I couldn't have not shown up."

Jessy had no idea who Suzi Quatro was, but she definitely agreed that Barry Manilow didn't rock.

"He sounds like a jerk," she said.

"Of course he's a jerk. He's a guy."

"Why should that make him a jerk?"

Twyla looked at her like she was an idiot.

"All guys are jerks," she said. "They just are."

"I have lots of friends who are guys," Jessy insisted. "They're not jerks."

"Sooner or later, they'll turn into jerks. They always do."

That didn't make any sense at all. She knew guys who were jerks already, and girls who were too.

"I think my friends are going to stay my friends," she said.

"I hope you're right about that. But things are going to get weird when people start dating."

"Some people are already dating."

Twyla laughed. "Mom would love to hear that."

The phone rang, and Twyla hurried to answer it.

"Hey," she said, and listened for a minute. "No, I wish I could. I have to babysit."

Silence on her end.

"I know. They just about died." She laughed.

"So now I have to work up some points again. No, she'll forget about it by the end of the week, she always does. It's a drag, though." She laughed again at whatever they were saying.

"I'm not going to miss that. No, that's okay. If you come over, they'll come back early -- yeah, I'm sick of everything -- no kidding. I don't know, I've thought about it. I don't really have any money."

The stove timer started to buzz, so Twyla got off the phone. She cut the pizza into slices, mock-dramatically, and they ate the pieces right off the cookie sheet, hovering over the stovetop.

When they were done, they washed the pizza pan, and left the metal mixing bowl to soak a while in the sink. They knew that their mom would expect the dishes to be done, even though it didn't seem that leaving them overnight would do any harm. But like Twyla said, there'd been enough trouble.

"Can we make popcorn for the movie?" Jessy asked.

"Why not? We're living it up."

They got the big, heavy black iron skillet from the low shelf by the fridge. The popcorn was in a big, heavy glass jar. Twyla put the skillet on the burner, and poured oil into the circle. She twisted it expertly, so the oil rolled evenly all along the bottom, and scattered kernels out of the jar into the skillet, like she was throwing chicken feed. Then she turned on the burner, and the flame floomped into a burst of blue.

At first, the skillet wasn't hot enough that she needed a pot holder for the protruding metal handle. She let it heat up, shaking the skillet occasionally, so the popcorn snaked around on the surface. Finally, the first kernel popped into a white blossom. She started shaking harder, and with the other hand, she reached out and grabbed the metal cover that fit on top of the skillet.

Before long it was popping and shaking and rattling, the bottom of it scraping the burner. By then, Twyla had grabbed a pot holder off the hook and wrapped it around the handle. The metal cover started to strain above the pressure of all the kernels, and it separated, so it didn't actually fit on the rim anymore, but had a noticeable gap. A flurry or two of popcorn escaped out the side and spat onto the stove top.

The noise grew more infrequent, just an occasional random, deflated-sounding pop, so she lifted the pan, heavier now, and settled it onto one of the unused burners. When she took off the cover, the skillet was full of bulbous white corn.

Jessy had already gotten a small saucepan ready and cut into a stick of butter. She used the knife to pry off a chunk and dump it into the pan. That had been heating up, slowly, at a low temperature, on the other side of the stove. She had stirred and stirred while it melted and slowly browned. Twyla shook the skillet around some more, like she was tossing a salad, to keep the kernels from burning as they cooled. Moving the saucepan the whole time, to coat the popcorn evenly, she poured the butter over the top, and stirred it all around.

For the finale, Twyla went to the fridge and took out the big green shaker of Parmesan cheese that they used for spaghetti. She shook cheese all around on the popcorn, and stirred it up again and shook some more, so the cheese stuck to the butter that stuck to the corn.

While Twyla rinsed out the saucepan, Jessy went to the cupboard and took out the box of cocoa, pulled out a packet, and smacked it against her palm. Then she picked up the tea kettle and jerked it up and down, testing how much water was in it, before flaring up the burner again.

Once the cocoa was ready, she took a single piece of puffed popcorn daintily in her fingers and dipped into her mug. As soon as it touched the hot liquid, it began to shrink and shrivel, so she had to rush it to her mouth before it collapsed. Delicious. Twyla poured a cup too, and they both did that for a while, a kernel occasionally shriveling too fast and dropping right into the cocoa. The disintegrated remains were so small, it was hard to fish them out.

Then they poured the rest of the popcorn into one of the biggest metal mixing bowls, and carried it into the living room, along with a whole roll of paper towels.

By the time the movie started, her fingers still slathered in butter and cheese, Jessy realized she was in fact perfectly willing to be scared. That probably meant she was going to get scared. But she wasn't going to admit that was any kind of problem.

The movie was great. It was set in a small town, that reminded Jessy of their own street somehow, like when they walked downtown, from the movie theater, at night. Not a city, like most of the TV shows she watched, but a normal street, with trees and houses just like their house. It was somehow scarier to think of scary things happening in a place that looked like where she lived.

"That was really corny," Twyla said, when it was over. "It would never hack it at the drive-in." She had taken over the Big Chair, the recliner that stared right into the TV.

"It was black and white," Jessy said. "It's old."

"Did I ever tell you about *Don't Look in the Basement?*" she asked. Just the title gave Jessy the immediate creeps.

"No."

"It played at the drive-in last summer. Now, that was scary."

"What was it about?"

"This girl gets a job working at this hospital, and it's a spooky building, in the middle of nowhere. And everything about it just seems a little bit -- off. Things aren't the way they should be, but you can't really put your finger on why. She's supposed to meet with the doctor, but the doctor doesn't seem to be there. And then it turns out, it's not really just a hospital."

Jessy took refuge in the popcorn bowl, distracting herself. By now the popcorn had cooled, which made the butter congeal on the buds, and the cheese specks stood out in the waxy coating. That's when she liked it best. There'd be a pool of hardening butter on the bottom of the bowl, and she scraped the kernels in it, covering them.

"It's a mental hospital, so all the patients are crazy. And you know that some of them are dangerous."

"Have they killed people?" Jessy asked.

"She tries to figure out what's happened to the doctor, but then people start getting killed."

"So, what's in the basement?"

"I'm not telling you that!" Twyla laughed.

"That's not fair! You have to tell me."

"You're going to have to see it for yourself."

"I'm never going to be able to go to the drive-in," Jessy protested.

Twyla just kept laughing at her. "What do you think is in the basement?"

"Is there a dead body in the basement? A skeleton?" She tried to think what it could possibly be. What could be worse than a whole houseful of crazy people, some of them killers? How could the secret be any scarier than what she already knew? She wiped her hands on the sheaf of paper towel, and then she picked up a small pillow from the couch and whacked Twyla with it. Twyla whacked her back, and they both laughed.

"Maybe they'll start showing more scary movies again this year," Twyla said. "We'll have to check the paper on Sunday. As long as you don't have trouble sleeping tonight."

"I'm fine," Jessy said, sullen. "It wasn't even really scary."

"We better wash the rest of the dishes," Twyla said.

"I'll wash," Jessy said.

"Really?"

"I don't like drying," she said. "It's more boring."

"I don't know if I could choose which is boringer," Twyla said. "When I leave home, I'm never going to wash dishes again."

"How will you eat?"

"I'll just use paper plates, until I become a rock star and start making lots of money. Then I can hire a maid to do it."

"Mom always says she wouldn't want to have a maid come in and mess up her things." This came up one day when the neighbor ladies were over. Someone they knew had hired a housecleaner, and everyone was disapproving.

"Yeah, right. If Dad would pay for it, she'd get a maid. And anyway, you don't think David Bowie does his own dishes, do you?"

"I guess not." The thought made Jessy giggle.

Shortly before their parents were supposed to be home, Twyla ordered Jessy to put on her pajamas.

"I want you to be ready at a moment's notice," she said. That was a good idea. The outside door always stuck when it was unlocked, making a horrible ratchety noise, so when they heard their parents elbowing it open, Jessy had plenty of time to run up the stairs and jump into bed. She heard Twyla tell them, sulkily, that it had been an uneventful evening. In a little while, her mom came up the stairs and peeked in Jessy's partly-open doorway, where she looked asleep under the covers.

Jessy lay awake until she heard Twyla come up the stairs and into her room, and then their parents came upstairs and went down their part of the hallway, to settle in for the night. Twyla put a record on, the sound down low. Jessy couldn't quite make out the song through the wall, but it was nice to hear anyway. Finally, after a long time, someone came down the hall, trying to be really quiet, and switched off the hall light.

Slowly, Jessy's room seemed to grow darker, even as her eyes adjusted to the light. Her white curtains and the pair of window shades behind them seemed to glow a little. She began to wonder if she was safer leaving the door partway open, or if it would be better to shut it, as much as she could.

It depended on where the scary thing was going to come from. If it was in her closet, or came in through the window, she needed easier access to escape into the hall, so she'd want to leave the door open. If the threat was somewhere in the rest of the house, then it would have to come in through the door. Even though there wasn't a lock on it or anything, somehow leaving the door wide open seemed like an invitation. I'm here! Kill me!

The house gave a faint creak, from somewhere distant, maybe the roof. Her dad always said it was just an old house, settling. It sounded for a second like its stomach was rumbling. Or maybe it was a faint footstep on one of the many creaky boards.

Not that ghosts had footsteps. So that ruled them out, at least for the moment, from the forefront of her worries.

She had just seen a movie about vampires, and vampires had bodies, and weight, and would definitely make a sound when they stepped on a vulnerable spot on a wood floor. Twyla would say that the movie was a little too scary for her. It hadn't seemed too scary at the time she was watching it, though, and you'd think she'd have noticed. You'd think it would be scarier when it was actually happening, and not hours later, when the details were already starting to fade.

Jessy knew she'd better get some sleep, or her parents would pay more attention to what she was watching. She couldn't have that, not so close to Halloween.

****

The girls stopped off at Jessy's house after school one day, and when her mom heard them come in, she met them in the living room.

"It's too early," she announced, "and I don't like it. But I give up. If I have to look at the neon spiders all day, we may as well get the Jack-o-Lantern Box out."

She rustled around in the deep closet, behind several square Christmas cartons, and emerged with a tall, narrow cardboard box - - it had stood in as a pretend coffin in Halloweens past -- with a worn, partly dented top. Twyla had drawn a jack-o-lantern face on the cardboard with magic markers, its sharp black mouth, almost in fangs, peering out of a scribbly orange face.

Jessy and Karma dug into it in the middle of the living room, pulling out all the fabric. First came a big, oblong piece of rough grey cloth they used as a shawl. It had been cut but not hemmed, so the threads along the edges pulled right off it. There was also a shiny black Dracula cloak, too short for them to actually wear as a costume, but good enough to play with around the house, and an old Indian maiden outfit, with a string of beads, a bedraggled black wig, and a gypsy-ish skirt made of thin, multi-colored material.

They found the ghost candle, who looked like a white wax sheet with eyes, holding a small jack-o-lantern. It had never been burned, but the surface felt worn out, rubbed-down, by time. An orange and black plastic scarecrow was next. He wore an open pack on his back, showing that he was hollow inside. They suspected he'd once been filled with candy, but Jessy's parents didn't remember where he had ever come from. Then the puzzled-looking white ghost mask, the elastic strap completely gone. It was funny how often the ghost decorations looked slightly befuddled, but then, it seemed logical that a ghost would be confused about what was going on.

Karma fished out a small plastic witch's hat, that Jessy usually put on the head of a small pumpkin, when they got them. Her mom wouldn't let them try to carve those ones, because they were too small; they'd pretty much fit in the palm of Jessy's hand. They had to draw on them with black magic marker, which seemed like cheating, for a jack-o-lantern.

Then they sorted and stacked all of the paper: the black cat cut-outs, the owls, the bats, the silhouettes of witches on their brooms, along with the patterns, cut out of card stock. Plus dozens of construction paper jack-o-lanterns: small ones a few inches across, big ones made of nearly an entire sheet, rounded orange paper, oval orange, oblong. On a lot of them, the paper was beginning to fade to a paler, grainier orange.

Twyla had made almost all of the paper stuff in the Jack-o-Lantern Box, and it irritated Jessy all over again how she'd gotten so scornful, like being too grown-up for trick or treating meant she had to turn her back on Halloween.

"Some of those are looking pretty shabby," Jessy's mom said, looking in on them. "You should throw them out."

"Mom!" Jessy was shocked.

They also had some printed, store-bought decorations on thin cardboard: black cat cut-outs, with cruel expressions and sharp paper claws; a skull in psychedelic colors, pink and yellow, with bulging, flaming eyes. And a handful of paper bones: Jessy took the longest one and laid it out, the length of her own skinny arm.

"It's Clarence, the Skeleton King!" Karma cried, pulling him from the coffin.

Clarence was a tall skeleton, with fuzzy green bones that used to glow faintly in the dark, printed over the top of thin black cardboard. His joints were marked with tiny round holes, rimmed with metal, so they could pose him in different positions: waving his hand, or bending his legs backwards into a jig. His neck was bent, though, and in danger of tearing, from having been used like a ventriloquist dummy over the years, his skull moved forward and back on the paper neck, to pretend he was talking.

Twyla swore it was Jessy who had started calling him Clarence, but she didn't remember anything about it.

They took the candle and the scarecrow, and the witch's hat, and set them up as a display on the living room end table. Then they got out the tape. Clarence and the other cardboard decorations went on the windows, so they could be seen from outside. And the things made out of construction paper went all over everywhere.

"How can it be too early?" Karma asked, as if she'd been pondering it the whole time. "The month's almost over."

"I know. If we got it out on the 30th I think it would be too soon for her," Jessy agreed. "Halloween is way too short as it is."

****

There was nothing on TV that night, so Jessy sat in the kitchen, listening to the big radio. It had a brown wooden frame and a fuzzy paneled front; she had no idea what kind of material it was. The window shade next to her was pulled down, and she felt warm and homey in the darkish room, in a small pool of light, still admiring her work with the cupboards, which were covered with pumpkins and angry black cats.

Suddenly she heard a sound on the other side of the window. A rushing, a whishing, then spattering. The wind had come up, and it was starting to rain outside.

Then a crack of thunder, abrupt and close to the house. Jessy opened the shade slightly, peeking out to peer into the darkness. The glass was blurred with water, and she saw a snap of lightning pop the backyard into bright, and then black again, leaving her blinking.

Her mom came rushing into the room, switched the radio off, then unplugged it.

"Mom," Jessy started to complain.

60

"You go upstairs, and unplug your sister's stereo. And all the lamps."

She was already going over to yank the cords of the toaster and the coffee maker out of the wall. When Jessy went through the living room, the TV set was already dark, and the coffee table light was dark too. Only the double-bulbed light on the wall, controlled by the switch, was still on. Everything else was already unplugged.

Jessy and Twyla didn't know anyone else whose parents made them unplug the appliances during a thunderstorm, but they always did. If they left something plugged in, they were just asking to be hit by lightning, although it wasn't such a sure thing as, say, taking a bath, or talking on the telephone would be.

Twyla wasn't home -- she couldn't get out of her youth group just by being grounded. So Jessy rushed upstairs, with her license to trespass.

When she went into Twyla's room and turned on the light, the overhead bulb flickered slightly, and she saw a big flare of lightning in the window, like it was just inches on the other side of the glass.

Maybe they'd get really lucky, and the power would go out. They had some old-time kerosene lamps, with glass tubes and glass bulbs, full of ruby-red liquid. Her dad had picked them up at auction sales over the years, and cleaned them up. Even when the power did go out, their parents usually wouldn't light them, but sometimes they did, and that was a big event.

Twyla's room was mainly a big pile of clothes in two corners, and a bed in the third, everything seemingly centered around the shrine of stereo against the far wall. All her records were in cardboard boxes, neat and in order: a big box for albums, a smaller box for 45s, and a couple of shoeboxes for cassette tapes. Plus all the usual stuff, like old stuffed animals, black light posters, an incense burner.

Come to think of it, Twyla turned on the black light about as often as her parents burned the kerosene lamps. At least when Jessy was around.

Jessy loved poking around in Twyla's room, looking for paperback books that she'd hidden, finding beers tucked away in the closet, sometimes dangerously borrowing her records and playing them on the smaller record player in her own room. Once, Twyla had come home before Jessy had a chance to put a record back, and she was jittery and nervous all the rest of the day. But luckily, she didn't notice, and Jessy was able to sneak it back into place.

She quickly unplugged everything from the stereo, with its tangle of connections in back, and tiny wires sticking out, twisted around other wires. She'd seen Twyla skimming the rubbery coating off the cords, exposing the wires and braiding them together, but she had no idea what Twyla was doing. Sometimes the sound would fuzz, and Twyla reached in back, sometimes wiggling and wobbling the wires, sometimes just a touch, and there'd be a crackle from the speaker, and it would all go back to normal.

Once she knew all the outlets were okay, she left hastily, turning out the light and shutting the door. Then she went into her own room and unplugged the little record player, and went down the hall to her parents' room, to unplug the couple of old-fashioned lamps with big glass shades that sat on their dressers.

The lights flickered again in the hallway, and the house felt like it was trembling, almost imperceptible, from the shake of the thunder.

When she got downstairs, her Mom had lit a candle in the living room and one in the kitchen. The light-switch light was still on; for some reason, their parents didn't think those were a magnet for lightning.

"Everything's unplugged," Jessy said.

"Good." Her mom settled back in her chair. "Thank goodness your father got the storm windows in." In the summer, this whole process involved closing all the windows, too, even when it didn't seem like rain was coming in.

They listened to the rain slam against the windows, the wind in a howl, a moan, a communication from somewhere unknown and unhuman. Her mom went back to her book, and Jessy started flipping through one of her mom's magazines. It wasn't as interesting as *Redbook*, but it was an October issue, so she hoped there'd be some Halloween crafts.

All they had, though, were the usual recipes, trying to make food spooky. Those always struck her as kind of corny. Food wasn't really a spooky thing, unless it was something you couldn't eat, like a cobweb-covered dinner plate on a dusty table in a spooky old mansion.

"Hey, Mom," she said, suddenly inspired. "Can we make cookies tomorrow?"

"Fine."

Eventually the rain let up, and settled into a gentle thrumming on the window. The thunder and lightning died down to a very distant rumble, the sky clearing its throat.

"Can I turn the radio back on?" she finally asked.

"I guess," her mom sighed, like she didn't really want to say yes. 'It seems to have moved on."

Jessy escaped back to the kitchen and turned on the radio. Somehow, having the music again made the room seem darker, like it was suddenly much later at night. Night in far-away Chicago, where it wasn't raining. She thought of all the strangers listening to this same music right now, while they lived their mysterious lives. What was it going to be like when she was Twyla's age, and then when she moved away and went to college, got her own apartment? She tried to put together some picture of adult life, based on magazines and songs and all the hours of TV she'd ever watched. All she knew was that life seemed to be very full of drama, and she couldn't really imagine any of it having to do with her.

****

Twyla and their mom had been in better moods all week. Doing the dishes the other night had probably done the trick. She'd already agreed to cookies, so after school, Jessy's mom decided they could get out the kitchen version of the Jack-o-Lantern Box.

It sat on a high shelf in the corner cupboard, the one with the giant rounded canister of flour, the smaller square-edged metal boxes of regular sugar and brown sugar, and the spices. All the special stuff was there, out of easy range: the box with the cookie press that only came out for Christmas, the small plastic shakers of red and green sugar, the krumkake iron.

Her mom gave her permission to stand on the tall kitchen stool, to get to the high shelf. Jessy stood on the stool all the time, but her mom didn't know that.

First she found the small box of cupcake spears: pairs of round black cat heads, green-faced witches with tiny pointed hats, and skulls. Then she carefully extracted a shallow rectangular box with a bright paper cover, orange and black, showing a witch's silhouette flying in front of the moon, over a scene of pumpkins and corn shocks, and a black cat with its back arched.

The corners of the box were a little battered, and it had some greasy patches where cookie dough had once stuck to it. Inside it were six cookie cutters: a bat, with its wings spread wide; a fat pumpkin; a cat, tail standing straight up; a rather lumpy witch; a broom, which was always the trickiest, because it was so thin that the cookies could snap; and an owl. The owl was Jessy's favorite. Or maybe the cat, or the pumpkin.

Her mom's big cookbook, covered with a red and white checkerboard pattern, was spread open on the kitchen counter, next to the clear sheet of waxy plastic, a little bigger than a placemat, that was spread open and stained with flour, ready to roll the dough on.

A couple of old Betty Crocker cookbooks sat out on the counter, too: the kids' cookbook that belonged to Twyla, and a cookbook especially for parties. Jessy loved to look through that one, with its line drawings of neat cartoon women in aprons, holding up measuring cups and electric mixers. The ladies in the cookbook were always entertaining guests, and serving meals with menus and courses. It could have almost been the same people from the *Orange and Black Book,* showing how they lived the rest of the year, when they weren't decorating for Hobgoblin Parties.

While Jessy mixed cookie dough, her mom made orange sugar, carefully dripping a splotch of red dye and one of yellow into a cup of sugar. The red was like a perfect drop of blood. But then she stirred it all up, and the vivid orange melted into the sugar. She rolled the cookie dough out into smooth patches, and Jessy attacked it with the cookie cutters, trying to fit as many cuts as she could on one piece of dough.

Some of the cut-outs they left plain, and some of them they scattered sugar on. Sometimes the sugar wasn't colored in the lines of the dough shapes, and in the oven it would make brown, caramelly burns on the cookie sheet.

They rolled up the remaining scraps of dough and squashed them together with more from the bowl. Jessy snuck as many clumps as she dared, when her mom was busy putting a batch in the oven. The raw dough tasted even better than the cookies.

Later, Twyla stopped in and swiped a few off the cooling rack.

"Orange bats," she said. "They match your pink spider."

"Smart aleck."

"I do make a fine cookie, if I say so myself," their mom said.

At school that week they studied bats. It was obvious that the teachers were starting to think about Halloween, too. The teacher handed out sheets of paper covered with line drawings of a bat, little numbers and lines pointing to the parts of its body. They talked about caves, and the definition of "nocturnal," which immediately struck Jessy as a useful word. She wanted to be a nocturnal creature, and she was sure she would be, if she didn't have to get up for school in the morning.

"I'm thinking about a story," she told Karma at lunch. "It's about a girl whose sister runs away and becomes a rock star." That was something that had popped into her mind the other night, listening to the radio after the thunderstorm.

"Why did she run away?" Karma asked, already excited. The brother of a kid they knew had run away, and it had caused a lot of excitement. Even though he wasn't gone long, it had practically turned them both into rock stars all by itself.

"Well, you'd have to leave to become a rock star," Jessy said. "And Twyla always says she can't wait to get away from here. And then she comes back on Halloween and helps the little sister drive some ghosts out of their house."

After school, they played pretending that they were cheerleaders, and they were going to a keg party after the game. All the boys were getting too drunk, and they had to keep their wits about them. Eventually, they ended up in a pretend field, like the gravel pits that Twyla always talked about, but the invisible boyfriends had disappeared, and they were mad at them anyway. So then they had to pretend to walk back to town.

Eventually they came to the spot where the hotel was, on the dirt frontage road on the west side of town.

"We could call for a ride," Karma said.

"Are you kidding?" Jessy replied. "I'll be grounded for the rest of my life if my parents find out about this."

Once they got safely to their make-believe house, they climbed up on Jessy's bed, their legs hanging over the side.

"That was a close call," Karma said. "I can't wait until we go to college. I'm going to date nothing but older men."

"I think I'm still a little drunk," Jessy said, flinging herself backward. Then they segued smoothly back to themselves and their real lives.

"Have you decided on a costume yet?" Jessy asked.

"My Mom wants me to go as a hippie," Karma frowned. "Just because it would be so easy."

"That's no fun at all."

"I know. I might as well be a hobo again." She thought for a minute. "I was thinking about Harpo Marx."

"That's a good idea," Jessy said, respectful. Last summer the TV channel from the city had played a week of Marx Brothers movies, and they watched them every day.

"Yeah, but it wouldn't be scary."

"It's hard to do scary."

"Yeah."

Not only did their costumes have to be something they could make themselves, but their parents had to approve whatever they came up with. They didn't want to waste a lot of time on an outfit and then not be allowed to leave the house in it.

They got out the Jack-o-Lantern Box and sifted through what they'd left inside it. Jessy toyed with the ghost mask, the innocent O's of its open mouth and wide eyes staring up at her. Even if they couldn't wear it, it shouldn't go to waste.

"I have an idea," she said.

First they hung the ghost mask on the front door, with a white paper cut-out of a ghost body below it, shaped with curves, like a two-dimensional sheet. That got them on a roll, so they gathered up scraps of cloth from the bag under the sewing machine, took the old grey cloak from the box, and stuffed the scraps into the middle of it. They tied around it with a piece of twine, so that it looked, roughly, like a head -- a raggedy, scarecrowy one -- atop a dangling body of uneven cloth. Then they hung it from one of the trees in Jessy's front yard, near the walkway to the house, with another piece of twine.

When that was done, they went into the empty living room to read *MAD* magazines. Jessy reached under the sofa, where the stack was, all the covers falling off. That's where they kept all the communal books: the hefty Christmas catalogs, that they'd keep until they got the new ones in November; the *People's Almanac*; the big dictionary with its thick, pebbly white cover. She pulled out the magazines and they sprawled out on the floor with them.

Jessy started re-reading one of her favorite articles, a mock catalog for hippies.

"Maybe a hippie isn't such a bad costume," she said.

"Yeah," Karma said. "If it wasn't just wearing the same clothes my mom wears all the time."

Twyla yelled in the door when she came in, and leaned down to see what they were reading. She kind of snorted.

"You don't even know what a head shop is," she said.

"I do so," Jessy insisted. She did, sort of, from reading about them in *MAD*, and from hearing Twyla talking with her friends. There was a head shop a couple of towns away, where they got the feathered clips they hung in their hair, and where Twyla had bought a t-shirt with a nickel-like picture of an Indian head and the word "Piute" on it, which she didn't really understand, although she pretended to.

"What are you going to be for Halloween?" Jessy asked.

"Still grounded." Twyla dropped herself onto the sofa, looking exhausted and exasperated.

"No, I mean it. Why don't you want to dress up?"

"Because I'm not a little kid. It's bad enough, I'll probably have to do the Trick or Treat for UNICEF again, which is so stupid. And then there's usually a party at the church afterwards, to keep us from going out and soaping windows."

"Are you going to soap any windows?"

Twyla glared at her. Jessy knew you that don't reveal your plans ahead of time, only afterwards, when it was a *fate accompli*, but she still thought Twyla could tell her. Last year, a bunch of guys Twyla knew had toilet-papered a bunch of teachers' houses, and they hadn't even gotten caught. Twyla claimed that she hadn't taken actual part in this, but Jessy didn't trust her at all.

"Listen," Twyla said, suddenly softening. "If you ever do stuff like that, stick to things that are annoying, but that don't do any actual damage. Like, soap on the windows will wash off, but shaving cream on a car is trouble. If you get caught, it's better to be a nuisance. That's not a real crime."

Jessy couldn't imagine her and Karma doing anything like that, but she nodded.

"And no fire," Twyla added.

"What?"

"Drunk boys and fire are a really bad idea."

Jessy nodded wisely. "I bet."

"One year, a couple of guys set a fire in Mr. Jensen's yard." That was the chemistry teacher, who was known for being really hard-nosed.

Jessy sat up and folded the magazine shut.

"Is the party really that bad?" she asked. "I mean, nobody I know is having a Halloween party. That sounds kind of fun."

"Did you ever read that Agatha Christie book?"

"Which one?"

"You know. The one with the bobbing for apples."

Jessy felt a little shuddery, but she didn't let on.

"I haven't gotten around to it," she said. She liked most of the mysteries that she'd read, but just hearing about the apple-bobbing murder creeped her out.

"All it does is get your hair wet, and ruin your eye makeup," Twyla said. "And it's dangerous, leaving those buckets lying around." Her voice sounded sly, because she knew what Jessy was thinking.

"Which Agatha Christie is that?" Karma asked, after Twyla left. They'd both read *And Then There Were None*, which had been just about as disturbing as they wanted.

"It's a mystery about a Halloween party," Jessy told her. "Someone gets drowned in the bucket of water, that they used for bobbing for apples."

She imagined putting her head over the water, thinking it was safe. Like when she was little and hadn't ever wanted to put her face in the water when she washed her hair. It had made her feel claustrophobic, knowing that she wouldn't be able to breathe, even if she really didn't need to breathe right then anyway. It was too easy to imagine someone coming up behind her and holding her head down.

"Did you see what they did to the tree?" their dad said when he got home. Their mom marched out to the porch and stared at it.

"What is that?"

"It's a hanged man," Twyla said, like it was obvious.

"That's the most morbid thing I've ever seen," their mom said, then turned to their dad. "Don't you think they should take that down?"

"It certainly looks like Halloween," he said, so it got to stay.

That night, Jessy pulled out her secret notebook, flipping past the notes on the merits of vampires versus ghosts, and the page full of potential titles: The Spiders in the Churchyard, The Phantom in the Snow.

It had always been easy before. She just sat down and wrote something. But for some reason, this year it was a lot harder.

She started to write a description of the little sister getting ready for trick or treating, and drinking a glass of pineapple-coconut juice. It was hard to describe, though, and that nagged at her. Then she wrote a little scene about a car pulling up, the big sister getting out of the car in a black leather jacket, her hair all big and teased-up, like photos she'd seen in Twyla's magazines. But she couldn't figure out how to fit some ghosts into it.

After her bedtime, she watched a shadow move behind the haunted house window shade. She stared at it for a long time. Tonight she wasn't hearing anything in the house, but imagined something outside, like the shadow was scratching at the wall, the way Cupcake did at the door when she wanted to come back inside. Jessy lay awake, while all around her, it just got later and darker.

Part Two

Johnny the Hangman

They didn't really plan it, but over the weekend, Jessy and Karma ended up walking with Twyla down to the cemetery. Fallen yellow leaves were stuck flattened to the street and sidewalk, like patterns stenciled on the earth. Jessy looked at the houses whose back yards went right up to the cemetery's chain link fence, so close to the graves. How quiet would it be, in a neighborhood where so many people were dead? That could be her bedroom, she realized. The girl in her story. In the back of the house, facing the dead people. It would be a great place to have your bedroom, because how creepy was that?

Jessy looked across the field of tombstones. The graves seemed so lonely, as if not just their lives, but even their deaths had been forgotten. The grass, slightly yellowing, was almost completely covered by the strewn leaves, which stuck to their shoes, dirty yellow and brown, as they kicked through the moist surface.

"It had better not snow on Halloween," Jessy said.

"I'm not wearing my winter coat," Karma said. "No matter what."

Many costumes had been ruined over the years by snowstorms. It was hard to plan something that would look right with a big winter coat and snow boots on top of it. And anything involving paper or cardboard, like homemade masks, and even paper trick-or-treat bags, could turn into a soggy mess after walking around in sleet.

"Some of us are supposed to come here on Halloween," Jessy confided to her sister. "It's kind of a dare."

Twyla rummaged in her denim purse and pulled out a blue cigarette lighter, full of watery liquid, and a gold tube with what looked like tobacco at the end.

"You shouldn't smoke," Jessy said.

"Don't start."

"You're going to die of lung cancer before you get out of high school."

Twyla laughed at her.

"Do you believe everything you hear?"

Because of the wind, Twyla had a hard time getting the tube lighted.

"Who are you guys going to the cemetery with?" she asked.

"Troy and Scott. And maybe Corey."

"Do Mom and Dad know about this?"

"Just that we're going trick or treating," Jessy said. She suddenly felt like she was sneaking out of the house to a keg party. "They always give me the thing about being too young for boys."

Twyla sucked on the end of the tube. "They may have a point."

"They're just my friends," Jessy said. "It's stupid. Anyway, they say that you can see lights in the cemetery at night, so we're going to see if it's true."

They walked to the far end of the cemetery, where the last rows ended in a stretch of solid lawn, with fields beyond them. Jessy kicked again at the built-up leaves on the ground. Then Karma reached up and touched a piece of old rope that was tied around a thick tree branch, like a friendship bracelet, and tugged at it slightly.

"You really shouldn't come here on Halloween," Twyla said.

"Why not?"

"Because it's haunted."

"It is not." Jessy was almost offended that Twyla was trying to pull something like that on her.

"Don't you know what that rope is?"

Karma worked at it, but it didn't come loose. It was knotted, with only the faintest nub hanging off it. Probably it had gotten wet, and the threads had bound together like a fist.

"It's just an old piece of rope," Karma said.

Twyla tapped the end of the gold tube hard on the ground and stuffed it back in her purse.

"That's the rope of Johnny the Hangman. Haven't you heard of Johnny the Hangman?"

"You're making it up," Jessy said. They'd watched movies together about the Boston Strangler and Jack the Ripper, and of course there was that episode of *Star Trek*. "Johnny the Hangman" wasn't even original.

"Seriously." Twyla sat down on the edge of cement block anchoring the VFW memorial, a cast-iron cannon that kids stuffed with candy wrappers and empty beer cans. "Johnny was a young guy who was hired to be the caretaker here at the cemetery. He raked the leaves, stuff like that. He was really sensitive, and people picked on him, but he wanted to be, you know, a guy." Her voice sounded sarcastic about the word "guy."

"So he'd try to get with these popular girls, and he'd ask them out, but they wouldn't go out with him."

"So he – hanged them?"

74

Twyla gave her the behave-yourself look.

"Meanwhile, there was a killer terrorizing the town. These young pretty girls were turning up dead, all over town. Their bodies were found hanging by the neck from trees, just like how they used to hang people in the old days, in the Westerns. Everybody was scared.

"One day, Johnny met a girl while he was raking leaves here in the cemetery, and she was really nice. They talked, and she started to come back to see him. She got to really like him, and he liked her. But he never asked her out or did anything to make the first move."

One tree creaked really slowly, empty sounding. Twyla pointed to a little padlocked shed next to the standing water faucet.

"You know that shed over there? There used to be an old house there, really old and small, like a shack, where the caretaker got to live for free as part of his salary. So that's where Johnny lived. One day the girl decided that she was going to make the first move, if he wasn't."

She paused, for dramatic effect.

"So on Halloween night, when she knew she could stay out late, she came to the cemetery to surprise him. In the dark, from a distance, she could see something going on by that tree, moving around. As she got closer, the movement seemed to stop. Then she saw Johnny in the shadows, stepping slowly away from the body of a girl that was hanging from that tree, right where that rope is."

They stared at the frayed end of the rope.

"It was too late, the girl was already dead. So the other girl snuck away, and she went to the police and told them she knew who the killer was. They came to take him away, and the story leaked out while they were questioning him. He was grabbed by the mob and hanged by the neck, from the same tree where he hung his last victim."

The wind blew around the leaves some more, gusted them around their feet.

"The sad part is, he was a total split personality. He didn't even know what he'd done."

"What happened to the house where he lived?" Karma asked.

"The city ended up tearing it down," Twyla said. "It all happened years ago."

"You're totally making this up," Jessy said. "If it had happened, we'd have heard this story before."

"Stick a needle in my eye," Twyla said. "It's bad luck to come here on Halloween."

****

After school on Monday, they went over to Karma's house, and Jessy called her mom. Karma's dad had left the old-fashioned wooden-handled rakes out in front of the garage, for them to rake the leaves. Traditionally, it could take them a long time, because they kept rearranging and disassembling the piles, and jumping into them.

They walked outside under what was left of the leaves. It felt like they were already in the country, even though the town did sputter out a little beyond, with a few rambly businesses visible, like the auto parts place, and a couple of warehouses with big dirt parking lots, with old, gnarled trees swallowing them up.

At the far part of Karma's yard, it felt like being in a Trixie Belden book, where everyone had horses, and gardens, and there were plenty of creeks and caves and apple orchards to explore.

Somehow their small town wasn't anything like that. They had friends who lived in the country, on real farms, and came to school on the bus, but that was different: cornfields, stretches of ground with cows on them, corners where trees had gathered into patches of woods. They couldn't just go out there and explore anything. Not only was the highway there, but everything belonged to somebody, and was marked off with wire. When she read the Trixie Belden books, Jessy imagined the country as being sort of like a state park, where you could wander around at will.

"I wish my parents would let me have a horse," Karma was saying. Sometimes they played back here, walking their bicycles, pretending the bikes were horses, and cleaning the mud out of the tire grooves like they were using a pick on a horse's hoof. Karma had all the Scholastic Book Club books about how to take care of a horse, and was always trying to prove how responsible she was to her parents, but they said it was too much work, and too expensive.

"My dad goes out to the farm every day," she griped. "There's a stable right there. I'd go out there with him and take care of it, and I'd help him in the garden."

"It would be great to have a horse," Jessy agreed, imagining riding every day at the old farm. She'd never even been on a horse, although she'd seen them at kids' farms, at birthday parties, usually just hanging around in a distant pen, taken for granted.

Karma suddenly gave Jessy a sly look.

"Maybe we could do a magic spell to get a horse." They'd been preparing what kind of spells they were going to do on Halloween night.

"We'd have to do more research," Jessy said. "There isn't anything that specific in my book."

The bent metal bands on the rakes scraped and caught on the earth. In some spots there were at least two layers, a drier, crispier one on top, each leaf with one papery side toward the sun, and then a softer, wetter layer underneath. When a rake ripped into one of those patches, the damp side turned over with a rich, mulchy smell.

Karma stopped suddenly.

"Let's play Johnny the Hangman," she said.

"Okay," Jessy agreed.

"How should we start?"

They raked and pondered.

"It could start with Johnny stalking his first victim," Jessy said.

"Who do you want to be?"

Jessy hesitated for a second. Then she said, "I'll be Johnny."

They started to act out a scene where Johnny watched the other kids, feeling left out, and then started stalking Karma, who was his first victim. An old rope clothesline was strung between two trees in the yard, with a loose end dangling from the knot, where it looped around the trunk. That would be a perfect spot to hang somebody.

Jessy stretched the rope end in front of Karma's neck. It wouldn't go all the way around, but she pantomimed like it did, and then acted out as if she were choking her. Karma really got into it, her body flailing around, gasping. Then she leaned against the tree, holding the rope symbolically in front of her own neck, stretching her head up, dead.

At first they pretended the garage was the caretaker's house, and then it was the jail. The garage was overflowing with even more pumpkins, and other stuff Karma's dad had brought in from the farm. The exposed wooden eaves were strung up with vegetables, vines hanging down in lanky blond strands, clumps of beans drying. A squat, old-fashioned barrel, made of round wooden slats grown thready and dry, sat in one corner, full of tomatoes. The card tables were stacked with summer squash, long and curved yellow; buttercup squash, pale and misshapen; and bulging green zucchini.

After a while they went back inside, and scrounged pieces of cloth from Karma's mom, to make magical talisman bags with. Jessy's was purple, like she'd originally thought, and Karma's was pink. She was doing a spell for love, but she wouldn't tell Jessy who it was for.

"I didn't know you liked someone so much," Jessy said.

"It doesn't have to be for anybody specific, does it?" Karma asked.

She had actually had a boyfriend last year. He just asked out of nowhere if she wanted to be his girlfriend, and when Karma said yes, then she was. Sometimes when a whole group of them went to a movie, he sat next to her, and he bought her a pop, but that's all it really meant. He never called her on the phone or anything.

After awhile, time passed, and it seemed obvious that they weren't "going out" anymore. Karma had seemed kind of uninterested in the whole thing, so Jessy didn't know why she wanted another boyfriend so soon, if she didn't have someone in mind.

Karma's mom stopped in, asking if they wanted a snack, and she had a surprise: a whole plastic bag full of real Tootsie Pops.

"I thought we could make lollipop ghosts," she said. "And what we don't use, we can give out on Halloween."

The thought of candy put up in high cupboards, that nobody could eat until the end of the month, seemed wasteful. If it were up to Jessy, she wouldn't wait to open her Christmas presents either. But it wasn't a problem, because they could easily make a whole bagful of ghosts.

Each Tootsie Pop got a piece of Kleenex, which they put over the top of it, like a magician's handkerchief over his wand in a magic trick. They pulled a few off with flourishes, just to joke. Then, with the Kleenex evenly in place, they tied the tissue with pieces of black yarn. The dangling sides created a floating cloak of little ghost-body.

While the girls dabbed little faces on them with a felt-tip marker, Karma's mom unraveled some more black yarn to tie up the ghosts with.

"Where are we going to hang them?" Karma asked. She always made an effort to make her mom feel included.

"What do you think?" her mom asked.

They walked around inside the house, and paced in the yard, making bracket shapes with their hands and squinting, like they were looking through a camera. Then they decided to tie them up in the trees that had grown up tall on either side of the front door, drooping slightly over the steps.

They tied longer strings of black yarn to the ghost necks, and attached them to the bare branches of the trees. With luck, the color would fade into the darkness better at night, so the strings wouldn't be so noticeable. Not that anyone was going to mistake them for real ghosts, but still.

****

It was time to get serious about costumes, so that week they made another trip to the dime store, to look at the Halloween stuff again. They'd been right the first time; none of the costumes were quite right.

The store had gotten in a few more cardboard decorations though: a bat with a mean, fanged face, that was almost too exaggerated, and a green, warty witch stirring a cauldron. Jessy liked that one because of the small toad lurking in the bottom of the picture. None of them were as good as the ones she'd already bought, that she admired on her door every night.

Then she saw the pop-up cat.

It was a small jack-o-lantern, bright plastic orange, with eyes and features indented and painted black, smiling the crooked-tooth smile. On the back, there was a small push-button. When she pushed it, the top of the pumpkin's head flew open with a sound like a squeal, or a squeak, and a little black cat head popped up from inside. Its slanted eyes and nose and whiskers were painted white. Suddenly, Jessy loved the pumpkin, the cat, the squeak. She had to buy it.

"What did you get now?" her mom asked when she got home. Jessy pulled the pumpkin out of the bag and popped the cat, and her mom said, "You spent your money on that? It's a piece of cheap plastic. You're just like your dad, both of you, always picking up junk."

"I like it," Jessy defended the pumpkin.

"It'll be broken within a week," her mom predicted.

The girls went up to Jessy's room. She pressed the little stub, and the pumpkin-top flew open, the black head jumping up with a squeak.

"Okay," they got down to business. "We agree, no gypsies and no hippies."

"Ghosts would be so fun, but the sheets aren't practical," Jessy mused.

Karma suggested, "Maybe we could make wings. Like when we made the angel wings for the Christmas program."

"That's a good idea. But we can't be angels for Halloween."

"We could make owl costumes. Or bats."

"Bat wings!"

"My dad has a ton of cardboard," Karma said. "I'll ask him to break some boxes down, and then we can get started."

Once that was officially decided, Karma told her about an article she found, about how to make a piñata, using a balloon and basic paper-mache.

"We have paper-mache experience," she pointed out. Last spring they made a model of the solar system, squashing rounded balls of paper-mache into the relative sizes of planets. Then they poked wires into them, and lined them up in roughly the right distances from a light bulb sun.

"I think there's some old balloons in the junk drawer," Jessy said.

They found one that seemed big enough, and then dug at the bottom of her dad's newspaper pile, found the oldest ones, and grabbed some to tear into strips. Out on the porch, they mixed some flour and water in a big metal mixing bowl, and slathered the strips with the paste. Then they blew up the balloon and covered it with the wet paper, smoothing out the gluey surface, until it had a solid layer, and added more on top of that.

By the time they were done, their hands were as stiff with sticky white as the balloon was.

They left it there on the porch to dry overnight, perched in the center of more spread-out newspapers.

Twyla came up to her room later just to ask, "What is that blob on the porch?"

"It's a piñata," Jessy said. "It's going to be a jack-o-lantern."

"And what's this?" She reached over to the plastic pumpkin, and used the tip of her fingernail to flip the tiny knob. The lid flew open, and the cat head jumped out.

"You're really putting a lot of work into Halloween," she said. Jessy shrugged.

"It's like when we talked about how Santa Claus is really everybody," she said. "We have to do the same thing to make it Halloween."

****

They'd never done such a big paper-mache before, and had no idea how long it would take the balloon to dry, so they were glad that it was already hard to the touch the next day.

First they screwed a couple of little holes in the top, so there'd be something to put a string through, to hang it up later. Then they covered the paper-mache with orange tissue paper. At the ends, they had to fold the paper in weird corners and tape it down extra, to curve it around the roundedness. They carefully cut triangles for the eyes and nose, and a classic pumpkin-smile mouth, with one square-edged tooth poking down, and one poking up. Once she'd finished taping the face onto him, Karma held him up proudly.

"It's Johnny the Hangman," she announced.

"Perfect! Now we just have to think of where to hang him."

Today they were raking in Jessy's yard, and once they got started, it was Karma's turn to be Johnny. She mimicked hanging Jessy, and then came up with a scene where Johnny thought he heard someone coming, and decided to hide the body temporarily. So she play-dragged Jessy into the biggest pile of leaves, saying it was a similar heap at the far end of the imaginary cemetery, and covered her up.

Jessy got out of the pile, and while they pretended she was still in it, they raked it back together again. Then they became a group of little kids who came across it, just sitting there, tempting and unattended, the dry leaves catching the sun. So they leaped into the pile, and found the dead body. They screamed and ran, scattering away.

"Do you think the body would be stiff?" Karma asked, while they were raking it all back together.

"I don't know." They both pondered. "I know they get stiff at some point. Rigor mortis."

"But then, they also ... decompose." That word made them feel shivery. "And then it's a skeleton in the end."

Jessy thought it over.

"There's a lot about dead bodies that I don't know," she admitted.

****

When Twyla came back from Yearbook, she invited herself into Jessy's room. First she tapped at the paper kitten-and-pumpkin on the door.

"These were a good find," she said.

She closed the door, and they both sat on the bed. "I was hanging out with Joe the other day," Twyla went on. "And I asked him about his grandma."

Jessy immediately sat up straight, intrigued.

"I guess when she was just out of high school, a friend of hers had a big Halloween party, that she and her sisters and all their other friends were invited to. The friend lived in one of those big houses along Main Street." Jessy knew that stretch of old brick buildings, some of them turned into lawyers' offices. They had huge oval windows and cut-glass porches, so Jessy knew these friends must have been pretty rich.

"The sister, the one who became Mrs. Peterson, the hermit, helped her plan the party, and they got the book I gave you, to order the decorations. Apparently the house was completely decked out from top to bottom. Every table had an orange covering, and there were streamers, and paper black-cat heads strung from one room to another, and paper jack-o-lanterns all up and down the staircases. Every window had a lamp or a pumpkin it. And there was a table in the back, full of every kind of party food you can think of. They worked on it for weeks." Twyla looked at Jessy. "Kind of like you and Karma do."

Jessy picked up the *Orange and Black Book* without even thinking about it.

"On the night of the party, a handful of kids worked as spirit guides."

"As what?"

"It was another idea they got out of a book. The invitations were on cards shaped like pumpkins, and they told the guests to wait outside their doors at a certain time, for a spirit guide to escort them. So people didn't even know whose house the party was at. Joe's Grandma was one of the guides. She had a costume on, but she wore a plain grey robe over the top of it, that covered her face, and she carried a lit jack-o-lantern. The guides went to people's doors and sort of beckoned them, moaning and gesturing with the light, and the people followed them to the party. She said some people joked around and tried to guess who they were, but they usually ended up pretty creeped-out.

"Then when they got to the house, it was all lit up with lights, and it was just total Halloween. Once the guests had all been fetched, the guides took off their robes in a back room and joined in, and they all drank punch and toasted the grim reapers who brought them together for such a great party."

"Look at this." Jessy pointed out an illustration, a slim, elegant drawing of a girl in a sharp, feathery mask, covered with little circles that were obviously supposed to be sequins. Her orange and black gown was a gauzy checkerboard, with a skirt that flared out. Jessy would love a dress like that, although she didn't have the figure for its shape.

"Yeah," Twyla said. "That's the other thing. A lot of the guests were wearing these paper costumes from out of the catalog. They must have looked beautiful in that old dark wood room, drinking punch out of fancy cups, with their masks on. The men had masks and some of them had costumes too, but not like bums and hobos and all the stupid things guys wear now." She sounded disgusted with her own time.

"I don't know why they even bother. Anyway, part of the whole point of the party was to do fortune telling. Especially about love. Joe's grandma was kind of independent, she was going to college, so she didn't have a boyfriend and kind of made fun of all the girls for taking it so seriously. Like a Halloween party was really going to tell them about their future, and it was going to come true. But her sister really liked a guy who was at the party, and she thought he might like her, so she was hoping that the fortune would turn out the way she wanted.

"They did a fortune-telling thing, where they walked one by one, up the stairs backwards, holding a candle. And when they got to the top of the stairs, in the dark, they'd look over their left shoulders really fast, and they were supposed to see the face of the person they were going to marry, in a mirror that was right there. Joe's grandma was downstairs, with some friends, when her sister went up, and then when she came down, she was obviously upset. Mrs. Peterson had done the whole ritual, and when she looked in the mirror, all she saw was herself. Now, some of the girls said they had seen guys, one of them said it was someone she knew, but she wasn't going to say who. Another that it was an unfamiliar face, tall, dark and handsome. A few admitted they hadn't seen anyone, and the hostess said they must not have turned around fast enough to catch the spirit. That was the excuse for why it didn't work, and I mean, it was all their imagination anyway."

"What happened then?"

"Well, when Mrs. Peterson just saw her own face in the mirror, she took it to mean that she wouldn't ever get married, or that somehow she was going to be alone, just herself, all her life. Joe's grandma tried to calm her down, and finally talked her sister into coming back to the party, but in a little while, the sister went into the kitchen, and she saw the guy she liked kissing another girl."

"Oh, no."

"So she told the hostess that she wasn't feeling well, and had to go home early. Joe's grandma took her home and tried to convince her that she was just being superstitious. They were getting ready for bed when they heard the fire alarm go off."

Jessy was breathless by now. "What happened?"

"One of the candles had caught something on fire. There was all that paper, covering every surface of the house. Everybody was wearing paper. It was a huge fire. The whole house burned down, and a lot of people got killed. The friend who had the party, and the boy Mrs. Peterson liked, and the girl he was kissing."

"Oh my God!"

"So that's how she first got the idea that she was cursed."

Jessy stared down at the book.

"How come this didn't get burned?" she asked.

"Joe's grandma had it," Twyla said. "She helped make stuff for the party, and she was going to give the book back afterwards."

"This belonged to somebody who died," Jessy said, solemn.

Twyla grinned. "You knew that," she said. "It was Joe's grandma's, and she's been dead for a couple of years."

"But I mean, really died. That's different."

After raking some more leaves in Karma's yard, and a whole new scene of Johnny the Hangman, where the mayor tried to talk down the angry mob, they gathered up the big slabs of broken-down cardboard boxes that Karma's dad had gathered together for them. They traced the shapes of bat wings onto them, and then her mom insisted on cutting them out with her special craft knife.

When that was done, they colored them black with poster paint, leaving each side propped up, separately, to dry. Later they'd string twine through holes in the wings, and tie them in place around their backs.

"If it snows, they'll still fit over our coats," Karma said, approving.

"We'll be fat bats. Maybe we drank too much blood."

"I wish we had fangs," Karma added.

"It would be great to have fangs," Jessy sighed. They practiced saying "Trick or treat," then sticking their teeth out in a snarl.

"We have to get our bags together, too," Karma said.

Some kids had the plastic jack-o-lantern trick-or-treat buckets, bought from the dime store, and some had the decapitated black cat heads. When Jessy had first seen them in the store, a few seasons ago, she had begged and begged her parents for one, but they said they were way too expensive for something she'd only use one day a year.

When they were actually trick or treating, and met up with some kids who'd gotten the plastic buckets, they seemed awfully small next to their grocery bags full of goodies. The cat heads especially seemed really tiny.

"It's the volume," Karma had said.

Sometimes their parents were right about things, even if they didn't know it. Jessy still liked the look of the jack-o-lanterns, who were both cheerful and kind of creepy with their blank painted smiles. But she didn't want to use them for their actual purpose.

So every year, she and Karma hunted up good-sized paper grocery bags. They tried to find ones with handles, but for some reason, those were getting rare. Instead, they took spare bags and cut them into strips, which they used to make their own handles for the bags. Elmer's glue stuck the homemade loops on the sides of the bags, and then they swiped Karma's mom's stapler to give them extra support. Then they worked on decorating them.

Jessy made a big paper pumpkin, with a face kind of like the one on top of the Jack-o-Lantern Box, to glue on her bag. Then she used Karma's mom's cardstock alphabet pattern to spell out "Happy Halloween," even though that was a lot of cutting. Everything on her bag was orange and black. Karma cut tombstones out of grey construction paper, using the edge of the paper for the bottoms. Then she made a few cross-shaped ones, taller than the oval-topped ones.

Neither of them said anything about what would happen if it started to rain, or snow. None of their homemade bags had ever survived long enough to make it into the Jack-o-Lantern Box, but odds were they'd at least survive the night.

****

"Did you hear about Halloween?" Kim said, the next day at school. She looked kind of bright and excited.

Jessy just stared at her.

"There are Moonies in town." Kim spoke the word with exaggerated dread.

"What are you talking about?" Karma asked.

"Moonies," she repeated, like the phrase told them everything. "You know what Moonies are."

"Of course we do."

They had a vague idea. Moonies were some kind of hippies, who belonged to a weird church group. They'd read about them in magazines.

"They're going around town, knocking on people's doors," Kim went on. "They're supposed to be selling flowers, but they have pamphlets and stuff."

"Were they dressed up weird?" Jessy asked. She had a picture in her mind of people with bald heads, dressed in robes, like monks. Hippie monks. Sometimes they had drawings of people like that in *MAD* magazine.

"No, I guess they were just dressed in normal clothes. They were acting like they were from a real church." Her face looked grim with disapproval. "But my mom says they're not a church, they're a cult. They're Moonies."

Already, Jessy was hoping that they'd come and knock on her door, so she could see for herself what they looked like, how they acted. She'd never seen anybody in a cult.

"Some people's parents don't want them to go out on Halloween," a boy was saying. "They're afraid that the Moonies are here to kidnap kids."

"That's how they get people into their cult."

"I thought they were going to do a sacrifice," another kid put in. That turned everybody silent.

"They're going to grab a kid who's out trick or treating, and they're going to sacrifice them. To the devil!"

"There's going to be cops all over, making sure nobody gets kidnapped."

Jessy thought about it for a minute.

"I never heard about the Moonies doing anything like that," she said.

"What do you know about it?" Kim's friend challenged.

"They have stories about them, in magazines and stuff. If they were going around killing little kids, wouldn't there be a story about it? If they were like..." She trailed off. Not like Jack the Ripper. "If they were like the Manson Family."

A hush fell over all the kids. She had accidentally freaked them out worse by invoking the name.

"If someone knew they were going to kill a little kid, they'd just arrest them," Karma said.

"Well, the Manson Family had to do it for the first time," Kim said. "They didn't get arrested before they started killing people."

After school, Jessy and Karma played basketball with Allison and Corey. Each of them pretended to be one of the girls who'd gone to the state basketball tournament last winter. Jessy picked one of the stars that Twyla went to parties with, because she felt like she knew her.

Then they went over to Corey's. She lived right next to the playground, just on the other side of a dense wall of flowerless lilac bushes. The air was cooling off, and they slipped their hands inside the sleeves of their jackets, but it still felt good to be outside.

They climbed up into the backyard treehouse.

"You don't think Kim knows what she's talking about, do you?" Corey asked.

"No," Jessy said, instinctively.

They were all a little quieter than usual.

"Do you know that girl who lives next door to Julie Anderson?" Allison asked suddenly. "She's older than us."

"Yeah, her name's Debbie," Jessy said. "She was in the Girl Scouts with Twyla."

"Did you ever hear about how she found a dead body?"

"No," the other girls said together, the syllable denying that she'd told them and also not believing it ever happened.

"You're making this up," Corey said.

"No, really. My mom knows her mom. There was an old man who lived in the house next door, on the other side. He'd lived there forever, so he knew their whole family. Well, Debbie's mom had baked a bunch of Christmas cookies, and she asked Debbie to take them over."

When Allison paused, it was totally silent. Just the faintest rattle of wind in the dry distant leaves.

"She knocked on the door, but he didn't answer. So she looked in the window, and she could see him, sitting in front of the TV. Football was on, and she figured he'd fallen asleep watching the game."

"Just like my dad always does," Karma said.

"She knocked some more, but he didn't wake up. Since Debbie knew him so well, she thought he wouldn't mind if she just went in and left the cookies for him. So she went right in and set them on the kitchen table. She didn't want to embarrass the old guy, so she was going to just tip-toe out again. But when she got back to the front door, she turned to look at him, and suddenly, she thought something might be wrong."

The wind picked up the tiniest bit, and then died down again.

"It was almost like she had a premonition. She stood in the entryway for a minute, listening to the football game blaring. Then she decided to go wake him up, make sure he was okay. So she walked quietly into the living room, around to the front of his chair."

She stopped, waited.

"And he was sitting there, dead."

"That is so a lie," Corey said.

"No, I swear, it's totally true. You can ask my mom."

Jessy thought about Debbie. She was a cheerful, sensible girl, maybe, in Twyla's opinion, kind of a goody-goody. It was hard to imagine anything strange or scary ever happening to her.

"I think I remember that guy," Jessy added, thinking. "Didn't he always used to dress up for Halloween?"

"Yeah," Allison said. "That's the guy exactly."

"He used to have his porch light on, and a jack-o-lantern on the step, so you'd know to stop there. But when you knocked on the door, it would open, really slowly." She dragged out the phrase "really slowly," so it was really slow.

"Inside, the entryway would be pitch black. Then he'd come out of the darkness, wearing this Dracula costume, with his arm in front of his face."

"That's right," Karma said. "Little kids would scream and run away. But if you held your ground, even if you were scared, and you said 'Trick or Treat,' he'd give you the best candy."

"Did you actually go to his house?" Corey asked.

"Yeah," Jessy said. That was one time Twyla had taken them. "When the door opens," she said, "Stand still. If you run away, that's when he'll get you." Jessy hadn't even known who "he" was, and for all she knew, he was a real vampire.

"When did this happen?" she asked.

"It was just last Christmas."

"So this will be the first Halloween that he's, you know. A ghost," Karma said.

"We've got to go trick or treat at his house," Jessy said.

Corey looked shocked. "You can't trick or treat at a house where someone died."

"For all you know, someone could have died anywhere."

"Just think," Jessy said. "What if you went to his house, and the door opened up like that, just like it used to, and the house was all black inside …"

"Stop it," Corey said. Then she looked off into the distance, in the direction of the cemetery, visible just past the baseball diamonds. It was getting dark, but light still stuck to the sides of a few tall crosses, so you couldn't forget what it was.

"Do you think he's buried over there?" Karma asked. They all gazed into the darkness, toward the silent tombs.

"Probably," Allison said. "Like I said, he's lived here forever."

Corey got up and shoved herself into an open space closer to Jessy, so her back was to the cemetery.

"You're not scared," Karma said.

"No. I just don't want to look at the cemetery anymore."

"It's still there," Jessy said.

Just thinking about the cemetery made them all feel solemn.

"My Aunt Shannon saw a ghost," Corey said.

"She did not," they scoffed.

"It was in the afternoon, just bright and sunny and normal, and she went into a room, and her sister, my Aunt Sally, was standing there. She wasn't supposed to be there or anything; she lived in another town. Just as my aunt was starting to ask what she was doing there, Aunt Sally just disappeared. She says it was just like watching a candle blow out."

Suddenly the quiet residential street around the playground didn't look any less creepy than the graveyard had seemed while they were talking about it.

"Later that day, they found out she'd been in a car accident, right at that exact moment. She was killed instantly."

"I've heard of that," Karma said. "It happens all the time."

"Co-o-o-o-o-o-rey," a spectral voice came piercing through the evening air. They all jumped a little, but pretended they hadn't. It was Corey's mom, hollering at them to come in.

The girls were disappointed, even though they were maybe starting to freak each other out a little too much. The creepiness felt good in Jessy's bones. It was weird, though, because it wasn't like someone telling the story of a scary movie they'd seen, which they did all the time. These were real people who had died, and someone she knew had known them.

But people died all the time. It shouldn't make so much difference, the fact that she had this faint line of connection to them. Especially since she didn't even know the dead people, anyway. But it made the whole idea seem realer. All those tombstones she loved, and under them, there were actual people. Just like someday, she'd be dead herself.

As they walked the short distance to the house, everybody laughing now over their own spooky moods, Jessy felt thoughtful. She never thought about it much, but suddenly, she was aware that she was alive.

****

On Saturday, when their parents were gone for the afternoon, Twyla had a couple of friends over, listening to records in the living room, on the big stereo. One song had a line about "smoking," which made them burst out giggling. Jessy didn't know why it was funny, other than that they weren't supposed to smoke.

Then they went into the kitchen, brought out a couple of cans of beer, and set them right on the table. Jessy had seen beer plenty of times, in the back of Twyla's closet, but it shocked her to see it there, out in the open, in the kitchen, in the afternoon, where anyone could see it. Even if nobody else was home but her.

Twyla took out the tall soda glasses they used for making orange juice floats, and for lemon sherbet and ginger ale on New Year's Eve. All the spoons were mixed up in the drawer -- the big spoons, the normal ones, and the jagged-edged grapefruit spoons that nobody ever used -- and she dug out a couple of long slender ones, good for tall glasses. With a big spoon, she scooped hunks of vanilla ice cream out of its cardboard box, and stuffed them into the glasses.

Then she opened one of the beer cans, which hissed at her, just like they did on television. Twyla poured beer into the glasses, using the long spoon to push the ice cream out of the way, getting the liquid all the way to the bottom, and sloshing evenly throughout the glass. A really good float had just as much juice or pop as it needed to suspend the ice cream in it, but not so much that it got runny, or as mixed up as a milkshake. The best was so that every spoonful had a clump of ice cream, coated with creamy -- beer, in this case.

"Want a spoonful?" Twyla asked.

Jessy had always disapproved of drinking, almost as much as the smoking. But she was intrigued by the innocent-looking glass of ice cream. And it would be great experience for when she and Karma played high school girls.

"Sure," she said.

If Twyla was surprised, she didn't give it away. Jessy took the long spoon and put it, very deliberately, in her mouth. Fortunately, it didn't taste anything like beer smelled, which was foul. It had a faint malty flavor, mostly covered up by the creamy ice cream taste. It reminded her of the cola floats that Twyla sometimes made.

"This is delicious," Twyla's friend said. "We should make these at the Freezy Stand."

"It would be worth getting fired."

Jessy waited until the friends had left, and the glasses were washed and put away, when Twyla was hanging out in her room. Then she knocked on her door.

Twyla's head appeared at the narrow opening, her body hidden. "What?" she snapped.

"Can I come in?" Jessy asked. If she knocked and asked permission, a little formal, like she was afraid Twyla would say "no," she usually said "yes."

"Sure." She opened the door all the way, and Jessy automatically scanned the room to see if Twyla had been hiding anything. If she had, it wasn't obvious. Twyla must have been sitting in front of the stereo, because there were records all over the place. Jessy dropped down on the bed and sprawled on her stomach, feet in the air, elbows hanging over the end, as Twyla sat back down on the floor.

"How's school?" Twyla asked. Jessy made a face, and Twyla nodded.

"I wish I could bring that guitar home," Twyla continued talking. "It would make it so much easier to practice if I had it here. It's such a crappy guitar, I don't know what he thinks I'm going to do to hurt it."

"He just wants you to go over to his place," Jessy said. Twyla looked at her, surprised.

"Maybe."

"Are you getting any good?" Jessy asked. This wasn't what she wanted to talk about, but she was interested.

"I don't know. Not bad. I wish I was better." She reached for a can of pop that was sitting on the metal stand by the stereo, surrounded by African violets in black pots, and geraniums in tin cans. "I really wish I had an electric guitar to practice on, but I'm working on it."

They chatted a little more, Twyla sometimes getting absorbed in looking through the box of records, which she seemed to be organizing.

"Have you heard this thing?" Jessy finally asked. "About the Moonies?"

Twyla snorted, and looked pretty amused.

"Yeah, what a bunch of BS."

"Really?" Jessy sat up.

"It's some hippie church, like the Love Gospel or something. They have one of those old school buses with peace signs all over it. Has-beens."

"I heard they're going to kidnap a kid on Halloween."

Twyla laughed out loud.

"People are so stupid."

"And they're maybe going to kill them."

"On an altar in the graveyard, with a special fancy knife?"

"Maybe."

Twyla looked her over. "They're not even in town anymore. They were just raising money to fix their bus to go to the Cities. And nobody's going to be sacrificed. I think someone's trying to scare you kids into staying home, so you won't get in any trouble."

****

For some reason, Jessy hadn't been able to work on the Halloween story. Her original idea had dwindled away, and she started writing a story about Johnny the Hangman. It would have a lot of characters in it, and her friends always wanted her to put their names into her stories. So she'd written a scene where a girl named Allison went to the cemetery, to visit a grave, and Johnny followed her home, and killed her.

When she looked over it again, she realized that all her friends' characters were going to get killed, and that would probably freak them out. She'd just been thinking of it as a story. So even though she thought it was starting out pretty scary, at least enough for a TV movie, she gave that up and started over again, with the sister becoming a rock star.

So now, sitting up in her room, fiddling with her notebook, Jessy tried to think of a way to get Moonies into a story. At this rate, she was never going to get anything finished by Halloween. She could barely get through her description of the little sister's bedroom, which was all hung with white sheets of paper, spiders and owls and cauldrons drawn on them in fluorescent crayons.

Maybe there could be a poltergeist, she thought. She and Karma had read all the books in the public library about real-life ghost sightings, so she knew that poltergeists tended to hang around teenage girls. Just like Twyla, she thought. She didn't know why that would be, but it seemed to be a fact.

She tried to imagine what it would have been like, when the sister disappeared. Even if she left a note, that wouldn't stop people from worrying. Jessy tried to imagine if Twyla really ran away. She could hear her parents fighting, blaming each other. Each time the phone rang, they'd get their hopes up that it was good news. Or be afraid of bad news.

So maybe the big sister ran away because the house was haunted, and the poltergeist bothered her, but nobody believed it. And the ghost was still in the house, waiting for the little sister to get old enough to trigger it again. Jessy thought that was actually a good idea, but making it happen all seemed really complicated.

Cupcake was asleep in her room, nose buried deep in a sweater thrown over the desk chair. Jessy ran a hand thoughtfully along her spine, and the cat adjusted her curl a little bit, hugging herself just slightly more, a paw shifted over one ear.

It suddenly occurred to Jessy that she didn't know how you'd drive ghosts out of your house. She kept thinking of holy water, but that was vampires. And vampires couldn't hide in a house for years, not without someone getting suspicious.

****

"Make sure to pick out a few pumpkins for yourself," Karma's dad said, while they were setting up his pumpkin stand. She and Karma walked around and around, picking some up, looking at them from all angles. Finally Jessy set a few aside. It was hard, because every pumpkin was beautiful in its own way.

Karma's dad had made some corn shocks, not to sell, but to use as decorations, to prop up next to the "Pumpkins for Sale" sign. He also set up the scarecrow, or scaredeer, as he called it, that had been out in the field, but it wasn't very spooky looking. It was just some wooden sticks wearing an old plaid shirt, with a bleach bottle for a head. When Jessy tried to imagine it moving on its own, or coming to life, it didn't seem any creepier than it would be if the vacuum cleaner did.

Okay, maybe that would be creepy too, but it wouldn't be especially Halloweeny.

The girls sat together at the card table, a plastic red-and-white checkerboard tablecloth draped over it, with the metal cash box, and a sheet of paper with the prices written down. Pumpkins and squash spread out on more card tables, and in wood and wire baskets, and piled on blankets on the ground.

Most of the day was busy, although there was a lull around the lunch time. They took a break and ate baloney sandwiches with mustard, sitting by the scaredeer.

"I wonder why they call them shocks," Jessy pondered.

"When I was little, I got lost in the corn field once," Karma said. "That was a corn shock."

They giggled at the bad pun.

"Really?" Jessy asked. "What happened?"

"It gets really tall, taller than you'd think. You start going in, and you can still see the houses and stuff, you can see through the stalks, so you don't think anything of it. But if you go just a little further, then you turn back and all you can see is a forest of corn. It becomes a wall, and it all looks exactly the same, so you don't know where you are any more."

"What did you do?"

"I kept going, looking for my dad. Then finally I guess I started to cry -- I was pretty little -- and I hollered for him, and he found me. They were pretty mad, though. They told me a million times not to go near the corn."

Jessy didn't ask why she had, because the answer was so obvious. Of course she had to go into the corn; she had to see for herself. That's why Karma was her best friend.

She rolled the word around in her mind. Shock, shock, shock. Like a "tic, tock," but with a whispery "Sssshhh" on top of it, like the sound the wind made, rushing through dry leaves. It was the perfect word for what it meant.

Throughout the day, people came up to the table and bought pumpkins. The sky was blue and clear, and the few remaining leaves were a perfect canary yellow, poised against it, like they were showing off. Everything smelled like earthy vegetables, like the smell when the pumpkin stalk was cut off from the vine.

It was dusk, and overcast, when they drove Jessy home. Karma's dad helped her carry in her pumpkins, and a bag with some clumps of shellacked Indian corn from the farm. A few of them were for her dad, to use as decorations when he exhibited his furniture, when he finished it. Jessy had already picked out the best one, a big cob covered with shiny black corn, and she hung that on the inside front door. She took a thick one, with mixed-up patches of red and yellow, and put it on Twyla's door, over the top of a decoupage sunset.

Her mom had gotten out the good candy dish, and tumbled and mixed together a bag of candy corn and a bag of the small candy pumpkins. Jessy nibbled a little chunk out of the tiny pumpkin, while Twyla and her mom wrangled over which knives they'd use for jack-o-lanterns. They ended up with the big kitchen knife for the main cutting, and steak knives for the details.

"Be careful with those," their Mom said.

The sky was almost fully dark when they went outside to work on the jack-o-lanterns. Jessy lingered for a minute on the front steps, watching the lonely hanging man twist slightly on his bare branch. The air was scorched with the smell of leaves burning nearby, and Jessy looked around, wondering where it came from.

Next door, something orange and black flicked in the Andrums' backyard. They had one of those old, chunky stone structures in their yard, like a fireplace that was missing a house. From a distance, they looked like stone huts, big enough for dwarves to live in. Jessy wished they had one in their yard.

She and Twyla spread old newspaper all over the picnic table. Then they selected their victims, setting them down purposefully, and drew pencil outlines of soon-to-be faces on the pumpkins' grooved surfaces.

Jessy's first pumpkin had a vaguely heart-shaped face. She tried to dig its guts out with a big spoon, but orange slime kept sticking to her hand. The smell of the innards had a sharp bite to it. Once she had it scraped down to the rind, she reached into the hollow and slowly pushed out the triangular chunks of eye. Little cut slits extended from each sharp angle, where she'd overshot with the knife, leaving narrow wounds, slashes in the corner of each eye. Her finger traced one, bothered by the flaw.

"No one will notice," Twyla said.

"Really?"

"All that matters is how they look in the dark."

Jessy made that one smiling, with big crooked teeth.

Twyla's first pumpkin had a wide "O" for a mouth, with matching rounded eyes. Jessy could never cut circles that well.

"This is going to be the scary one," Jessy said.

"Mine too."

They ended up with slanting eyebrows and angry, jagged mouths, ready to bite.

Jessy carried the bag of guts back to the garbage can, past the thornier bushes, and the short trees with empty branches. She paused. In a story, she thought, that's the point when she'd hear an owl hoot, or see a shadow rush toward her, from the alley.

Turning back toward the house, the pumpkins looked good and spooky on the steps. The flickers of candle were like small, dark flashlight signals, Morse code. Maybe because they were in the mouths, it seemed like they were trying to speak. If a jack-o-lantern cleared its throat and spoke, that would definitely creep people out. And what language would a pumpkin speak, if it did?

It was starting to get cold. Jessy thought about hayrides and hot apple cider, and bobbing for apples, but without the murder. She didn't really have a clear picture of hayrides, except that horses pulled wagons, and people sat in them, on top of hay bales. It sounded vaguely like the barn dances they had in old books, which she guessed were the same as any other kind of dance, only in a barn. She'd never heard of one happening around here, even from kids who lived in the country.

Reading books, it always sounded like people used to have more fun, but if that were true, she didn't understand why they would stop.

If she were a grown-up, and had a place like Karma's, she'd have an old-fashioned hayride and barn dance. In real life, though, it would be all the same people she knew, the same kids from school. Somehow that wasn't the way it was, when she thought of those stories.

Come to think of it, that seemed like it would be a good setting for something spooky to happen, in a barn lit by jack-o-lanterns. People would come expecting to be pretend-scared, but then they'd get scared for real. Like a horse and buggy, trotting along, slowly, and suddenly in their path there'd be a body, hanging from the darkened branches. Kids would scream …

Back by the house, Twyla was sitting on the picnic table, watching the eyes and mouths glow. Jessy sat down next to her.

"When I'm rich," Twyla said. "I'm going to buy a haunted house."

"What kind of a haunted house?" Jessy asked.

"A real one. A big one. With a real ghost." She stretched and leaned back a little. "You can come stay with me, at least part of the time."

"Would you be able to see the ghost?"

"I guess it depends on what's on the market at the time. Preferably one with a visible ghost, floating up and down the staircase. But I guess I could settle for mists and, you know. Creaking sounds. If I have to."

****

Jessy and Karma had mentioned the *Orange and Black Book* to the other girls, when they were over at Corey's house. They were all especially interested in the fortune telling, so they came over after school, stopping to call their moms, and then gathering in Jessy's room.

"Have you ever done the apple thing?" Corey asked, looking up from the *Orange and Black Book*'s description of throwing nuts into the fireplace, while you recited letters of the alphabet. "We did it once in Brownies."

Jessy shook her head. "I've read about it," she said.

"You're supposed to peel the apple in a big long string, and then throw it over your right shoulder. It's supposed to fall in the shape of a letter, and that's the initial of your one true love," Corey said. "But the peels kept breaking off so short, there wasn't much to make a letter out of."

"There's also a thing where you put something on your pillow," Jessy said. "And you dream about the man you're going to marry."

"I don't know," Karma said. "A dream doesn't seem like real evidence."

"Not like an apple peel."

"You know what I mean. I think you're more likely to dream about who you want to dream about. It's not – objective."

"You have a Ouija board, don't you?" Corey asked. So before long they were sitting around it, asking who Corey was going to marry. It spelled out Terry Anderson, who was in their grade, but had a different teacher this year.

"I didn't move it, did you move it?" they all asked each other.

Corey just muttered that she didn't believe in the Ouija board anyway, so they couldn't really tell what she thought of Terry. Then they asked who Karma's future husband was going to be.

"Chris Dole," the board told them.

Everybody laughed.

"That's not so bad," Jessy said. "He's kind of cute."

"Not cute enough to get married to."

"I could feel someone pushing on it," Allison said.

"Well, it wasn't me!"

Nobody would admit to it, and they were almost arguing. They didn't notice that Twyla had come out of her room, and was watching them from the doorway.

"You guys all think you're going to marry kids in your class?"

They looked up at her. "What do you mean?" Jessy said.

"You're going to live in the same town forever, you're never going to meet anybody new?" Twyla asked.

She turned to go down the stairs, and they all looked at each other. When they did another round, asking who Jessy was going to marry, it said she'd marry someone named Rick. Nobody could think of a Rick that they knew personally.

"So what are you doing for trick or treating?" Karma asked.

Allison made a face. "I have to go out with my little sister, and a bunch of little cousins. It's like baby-sitting, without getting paid."

"What about you?" Karma asked Corey. "You're still coming trick or treating with us, aren't you?"

"Are you still going to go to the cemetery?" she asked.

Jessy and Karma exchanged glances.

"Yeah, we are," Jessy said. Corey got the slightest excited-looking expression, like she was glad they were, but didn't want to admit it.

"Okay," she said.

****

During Reading, Mrs. Halvorson finally passed out small, thin paperbacks with the "Legend of Sleepy Hollow" story in it, although everybody called it "The Headless Horseman." Jessy knew it was famous, and she'd seen cartoons about the Headless Horseman, but she still thought it was kind of boring. It was too old-fashioned for her.

After school, they made carameled apples. Jessy's mom had bought something new, a plastic package that came with flat sheets of caramel, and a bundle of sticks. She complained every year about making them in the saucepan, because no matter how much they stirred, the caramel still stuck to the metal pan. It took forever to scrub off, and even though it smelled so delicious, and tasted good, the caramel remains got really gross, mixed in with the froth of dish soap in the murky water.

This was supposed to be easier, and Jessy had nagged her mom to buy it, when they saw it in the store. They spread out a thin sheet, and stuck the bottom of an apple right in the center of it. Then Jessy wedged a stick in the apple, pushing it in as far as she could, feeling the soft flesh give way. They pulled up the corners of the sheet, like they were making a running-away bundle, and tried to shape it around the apple. It didn't really want to stick, and it looked funny, like a badly-wrapped Christmas gift.

"The caramel's better when it's all hot and melty," Jessy said.

"Yeah," Karma said, looking at it dubiously. "It isn't really the same." But they made a few more and ate them anyway.

"You know, when Mrs. Halverson was passing out our papers today, I realized something," Karma said.

"What?"

"Chris's name is spelled D-O-E-H-L, not D-O-L-E."

"I always thought it was D-O-L-E."

"Me too, but it's not. You know what that means."

"What?"

"When we did the Ouija board, it thought his name was spelled the way we thought it was spelled. Not the way it really is spelled."

Jessy pondered over that for a minute.

"So you think that means we were really moving the thing, without trying to?"

"The planchette," Karma corrected.

"Right, the planchette. I guess that makes sense." She thought it over for a minute. "But how do you know the spirit knows how it's spelled?"

"Well, it's a spirit. It's coming from the other side. We ask the Ouija board questions because it's supposed to know things."

"That doesn't mean it can spell."

When Jessy went downstairs to watch TV that night, she could hear her mom and Twyla fighting again in the kitchen.

"I know you've been out drinking with those friends of yours," her mom was saying.

"I have not," Twyla said, vehement, the "not" crying out of the sentence.

"I'm just telling you now, if you get arrested, we don't have the money for a lawyer. If you get in trouble, you're on your own."

"Good," Twyla said. "I don't want any help from you."

Jessy didn't know if they knew she could hear them, or if they cared. It was hard to tell. It was probably best to ignore them, anyway, so she went over and switched the TV set on. It hummed a little as it warmed up, and the picture faded in.

"And just because your father spoils you, doesn't mean he's going to say anything different."

Jessy turned the dial to where her show was coming on, and settled back on the couch. She knew her mom and Twyla could hear the TV from the kitchen, and they weren't lowering their voices, so she couldn't be accused of eavesdropping. But she could still hear every word they said.

"I don't know why you have it in for me," Twyla said. "I'm not doing anything wrong."

"I think it might be better if you stayed home on Halloween," her mom said. "Or you can go to the party at the church. Or take Jessy trick or treating. But you're going to be home early, and you're not seeing your friends."

"Mom!"

Hearing her name perked Jessy right up. You couldn't go back from trick or treating by yourself to having someone watching you. People would think she was scared, which was ridiculous, or that her parents still treated her like a baby. Of course, sometimes they did, but no good could come of anyone knowing that.

"You're being ridiculous," Twyla went on. "Halloween is no different from any other night of the year."

"I'm not stupid. I know what you kids get up to. It's always better to avoid trouble than try to get out of it later."

"I'm going to watch TV," Twyla said, dismissive.

"Fine," their mom said, sounding completely unconcerned. "But I'm serious. You're not roaming the streets on Halloween night with a bunch of troublemakers. I want to know what you're doing and where you're going, and who you're hanging out with."

Twyla stomped into the living room, looking flushed and angry, and threw herself down into the Big Chair, fuming. Jessy thought for a good minute, and then stared ahead at the TV when she spoke, as casually as she could. "You could take us trick or treating. Me and Karma wouldn't mind."

Twyla glared at her.

"It might be fun. You know, like the last time you took us." She tried to make that sound meaningful, hoping Twyla would remember. That was the last year Jessy had gone out with a chaperone. Twyla took them to a half-dozen houses, including the dead Dracula man's, and then she went off with her friends, leaving the girls by themselves. They had roamed all over town alone. It was perfect.

"Well," Twyla said. "It would be a nightmare, but better than going to church." She scowled. "Or hanging around here with Mom and Dad."

Jessy felt pleased with herself, because she knew she was offering a useful alibi. She felt like she had the upper hand, at least for a little while.

Trick or treating with Twyla was actually one of Jessy's earliest memories. They went out early, so it wasn't quite dark, but only slightly dusky, the sky vaguely dim behind the dead bare branches of the trees. Jessy couldn't remember ever going outside at night before, and everything felt different, smelled different. They probably only went to the end of the block, but it had felt so strange to walk up to strange doors and ring the bells.

"Hey," Jessy asked. "Do you remember one time, when I was really little? I remember going into the stores to trick or treat. Did they used to do that?"

"There was one year, after we first moved here," Twyla said. "I can't believe you remember that."

"We went to the dime store. I remember they gave us full-size candy bars, but they had polar bears on them. I don't know what kind of candy that is. They were chocolate, though. Maybe a little bit like a Three Musketeers."

"The dime store, the drug store, and I think the grocery store gave out candy," Twyla said. "You didn't dream it."

"I wonder why they don't do that anymore."

"That was kind of fun," Twyla admitted. "It was like, we went to the store, but they treated us differently. They were actually friendly. But it's always more fun to trick or treat all over town."

****

Jessy's bat wings hung from the hook on the closet door, and her trick-or-treat bag sat ready in the middle of her desk. She popped the pop-up cat, listening to the squeak as the head sprang into existence. The transistor radio sat next to the bed, the sound turned down low. It was her last chance to get a story written this year.

Maybe the ghost was a girl who lived in the house a long time ago, when it was still a little railroad town, full of old wooden buildings and brick stores, like the ones downtown that had new siding and signs on them, but had been there forever. Her own house was an old house too, that had been there almost a hundred years. Or anyway, that's how old Twyla said it was.

All she had so far was a page's worth of fog, and the moon barely visible in the mist. And the trees were bare, and the leaves were past the point they were at now, all dry and crumbling into dust and nothingness when people stepped on them.

When the fog thickened, the vampire appeared, and then, when it dissipated, he blew away, like a billow of snow in a snowstorm. That idea seemed kind of nice. She didn't know yet if he were old, or pale, or cute, so she left him mysterious, his face hidden in the shadows where he lurked. He would watch kids like her, walking by the cemetery and he'd be disapproving. Would he grab the girl and just drink her blood and kill her? Or would she get turned into a vampire? And if she got turned into a vampire, would everybody be able to tell right away?

The especially creepy thing about vampires, and werewolves, too, was that they bit people, and then those people became vampires and werewolves themselves. It didn't seem fair.

Finally, she got out her special plastic-wrapped pack of loose-leaf paper, and she took her pencil, and started writing the story straight through, from beginning to end, like she always ended up doing, no matter how much she thought about it beforehand.

It was set in one of the houses next to the cemetery, with that thin line of alleyway between them. There had been all these murders, and someone in the story mentioned it being like the ghost of Johnny the Hangman.

"That's just a story," the main character said. "That never really happened."

"But a vampire, you'll believe that."

"Facts are facts."

The heroine realized that her little sister's boyfriend was the vampire, so she ran over to rescue her. She was wearing a necklace with a cross on it, but had it tucked under her shirt, so the vampire wouldn't notice. When she got there, her sister was hypnotized, like people always were in vampire movies, and the boyfriend was about to bite her, when the heroine cut open her palm and held it out, tempting him, and drawing him away. Then she pulled out the cross and burned him with it, giving them a chance to escape.

****

On Halloween morning, Jessy handed the story to Karma, who tucked it into her folder, and read it during Free Reading.

Karma thought it was really good, or at least she said she did. "It's just like a movie," she said. Jessy said "thanks," but really she was disappointed. It wasn't what she wanted it to be. She hadn't even gotten the pineapple-coconut juice into it, and somehow the sister didn't seem like a rock star at all.

They talked about the Headless Horseman in class, and what everybody thought happened to Ichabod Crane. Mostly the kids fidgeted, full of their plans for that night. In the afternoon, the teacher handed out heavy plastic bags, with a black and white drawing of ghosts printed on them. One of the grocery stores gave them to the school to give away, along with handouts about trick-or-treating safety, as if they hadn't heard all that before. Jessy had never seen anyone carry a flashlight on Halloween, but every year, that was on the list of things they were supposed to do.

As soon as school was over, they hurried home. Walking in the door, before she could even yell that she was home, Jessy was surprised to see her mom right there, sitting at the rarely-used dining room table, having coffee with their next-door neighbor, Mrs. Andrum. She was an old lady, but she and her husband never yelled at kids when they ran through their back yard.

"Say hello, like a young lady," her mom said. "Mrs. Andrum brought over some pumpkin bread."

Jessy didn't really like the taste of pumpkin, and anyway, that wasn't what they were for. But she said hi to Mrs. Andrum, politely, and went into the kitchen for an owl-shaped sugar cookie, not interested in what they were talking about. Suddenly she overheard Mrs. Andrum saying "The Halloween Fire was a terrible thing. I was too young, but my sister Anna went to the party."

"Oh, that's awful," her mom murmured.

"She left before it happened, thank God."

Was it possible that Twyla wasn't making something up? If that was true, then Jessy didn't know what to believe.

Her costume was ready, and Jessy was impatient to get started. Eventually she got out her most recent Scholastic Book Club book, a bunch of real-life ghost stories, with a spectral line drawing on the cover, white ghost over pale blue. She'd saved it to start reading on Halloween, and the stories were good, but she kept stopping to check the clock, and look out the window.

Her mom bustled around, filling up a big bowl with candy and setting it by the door. Jessy changed into her black pants and black turtleneck and black sweatshirt, and paced around. It was a lot worse than waiting for Santa.

At last, Karma's parents dropped her off. They fussed over each other's costumes, opened up their paper bags, trying to make the folds in the bottom good and firm, and reminded each other about their talismans, which they both had, in their pants pockets. By the time Corey walked over, dressed in a store-bought Supergirl costume, the air was getting dusky. They helped each other on with their batwings, and got ready to go.

Twyla went out to light the jack-o-lanterns, and their mouths pulsed with the flames. They left the house, excited, as if they were going to fly away down the sidewalk, with Twyla walking a few feet behind them, her hands stuffed into her jacket pockets, looking annoyed. They heard a bird call, lonely sounding.

"Is that an owl?" Jessy thought out loud.

"It's a mourning dove," Karma said.

"It's just a pigeon," Twyla said. "They live at the school."

She ditched them at the end of the block. They'd already planned out their cover story, about how they got separated.

"Don't get in any trouble," Twyla said. "Or you'll pay for it."

Their first house was Mrs. Andrum's. "Trick or treat!" they cried out, merrily. It seemed like she gave them especially big handfuls of candy, probably because she knew them. The next few houses had the front lights turned off. Dusty-looking leaves whispered on their grey lawns.

"Maybe they just forgot to turn the light on," Jessy said. That's how Twyla had taught her to trick or treat, going to every door. It was as an excuse to be out at night, to go right up to strangers' doors, as much as it was about getting candy.

"If they don't have the lights on, it's a waste of time," Corey said.

"We'll get more candy if we only go to the houses with lights," Karma agreed.

"Fine."

They went to the next house, which was split in half, two separate front doors sharing the same front steps. Both sides had visible windows, with lights on in each direction. They jostled to fit into the space, with their wingspans, and when they pushed the doorbell, they could hear the sound of bustle inside.

"Trick or treat," they called out when the door swung open.

Standing there, looking puzzled, was a girl wearing an enormous t-shirt and no pants, her hair in curlers. She wasn't much older than Twyla.

"What do you want?" she asked.

The girls stood there, equally confused.

"Trick or treat," Jessy repeated, in a plain, factual voice. The girl turned her head to face the room behind her.

"Is it Halloween?" she asked. Someone out of sight laughed.

"I think it is. I completely forgot."

The door opened wider, and another girl walked over to look at them. She had on a terry-cloth bathrobe, and makeup that was obvious in the bright light.

"Do we have any candy in the house?" the first girl asked.

"I don't think so, but let me check."

They all stood there awkwardly, and Jessy looked around at the room. Posters of enormous flowers, in big, primary colors, hung over a floral sofa, cluttered with pillows and magazines. These girls went to the tech school, and rented this side of the house. They were probably getting ready to go out, maybe on dates. Jessy could hardly imagine a more exotic life.

"Sorry," the girl said. "We don't have anything."

"Here." The other one grabbed a giant purse and rooted around in it. She threw a dollar bill in each of their bags.

"We'll have to turn the lights out," she said. "I don't have anything else."

"Thanks," they all chorused. They waited a minute, looking at each other, before they rang the other door. This was a well-known neighbor, and she oohed and aahed over their outfits, but was stingy with the candy.

"Is that what happens when you grow up?" Karma asked on the sidewalk. "I mean, how do you forget that it's Halloween?"

At the next house, a whole family of pumpkins clustered, burning orange on the front steps, and those neighbors threw candy into their bags. The morsels thumped on the bottom.

They were heading in the direction of the Murder House.

"Come on," Jessy said. "It's right there."

Karma and Corey stared at the house, its windows dark inside the nest of dark branches.

"Maybe later," Karma said.

Before long they crossed paths with other groups of kids, and bumped into Allison, who was dressed as a scary witch, with green eye shadow all over her face. She was holding hands with a very shy-looking little princess, who tightly gripped the black strap of her pumpkin bucket. They all talked at each other at once, and finally went in different directions.

"She always has such great costumes," Jessy said, mildly jealous.

"Her mom is a really good sewer," Karma said. "And I bet she did her makeup."

They went all through the neighborhood, and noted when they hit their favorite houses. Jessy sometimes pretended she lived in a particular house with a zigzaggy walkway, winding through a set of stucco squares, like ground-level chimneys, with bushes sticking their heads out of them. When the door opened, they could only get a look at the entryway, which looked like every other entryway, but she suspected the rest of the house was really interesting.

Karma liked to pretend that she lived at a cream-colored, cottage-like house around the corner, with a gate and an arched doorway. From the front you could see a whole garden curving around into the backyard, and a weeping willow tree. That house was on the same block as the dead Dracula guy's, but his didn't have any lights on, and it looked like nobody was there.

They knocked at the corner house that stood at a strange angle to the sidewalk, diagonal to the rest of the block, and at a small one-story house that looked like it was made of tin. Further up and down the block, they could see shadowy clumps of kids.

Eventually they wandered down a residential street, far from their own. They didn't know anyone who lived around there. Most of the porches were dark, and they didn't see any other trick-or-treaters. They stopped for a minute, and reached into their paper bags. Jessy's mom always made them swear not to eat anything until it could be inspected by adults, so after each of them unwrapped a candy piece, they automatically stuffed the wrappers into their pockets.

One of the houses had a light on, visible through the window, but there were no jack-o-lanterns or decorations or outside lights. They stood next to the door, trying to decide, when they heard a guy yelling at somebody inside. It sounded like an argument about who told who to clean this mess up. Karma made a face that they all agreed with, and they tip-toed back down from the steps.

When they had trick or treated everywhere they could think of, Jessy and Karma and Corey stashed their candy in Corey's garage, a bristling tangle of tools and looped hoses that stuck out in every direction. Then they went to the playground.

Big, theatrical lights hung over the small outdoor basketball court. On the far side, they could see the boys on the swings, just sitting and swaying, with two girls from school they kind of made fun of, for being too stuck-up to wear their glasses. They wore them to school, so their parents wouldn't know they took them off and stashed them in their desks as soon as they got there.

They never even talked to Jessy, but she still knew the story about how their parents wouldn't let them get contact lenses until at least junior high, and how it was really unfair. But contact lenses were really expensive.

Scott had a vampire cape, and Troy was wearing white pants and a white turtleneck. One of the girls had a big coat on, and a cowboy hat on her head. The other was wearing a long skirt, a mask dangling in her hand.

"What's up?" Jessy asked.

"We bumped into Tracy and Michelle," Troy said.

"Hi," Tracy said. Michelle just looked at the ground.

"They don't think we dare go into the cemetery at night, not on Halloween," Scott said.

Show-off, Jessy thought, but she didn't say it out loud.

"What are you?" Corey asked Troy.

"I'm a ghost."

"That's not what a ghost looks like," she said.

"Have you seen one before?" he asked.

Michelle didn't want to go to the cemetery, so Troy said he'd stay with her.

"You still wanna come, right?" Jessy asked Corey.

"Yes," Corey said, definite.

"Good." Jessy grinned at her, and Corey smiled back. It was obvious that Corey felt braver because someone else was scared.

The gates at the cemetery's main entrance were closed, but they weren't sealed off all the way. They were just long metal barriers, so nobody could drive a car in after hours, but a person could walk right around them.

It all looked different at night. Dry branches scuttled overhead. As they walked deeper and deeper into the cemetery, Jessy wasn't really sure what they were looking for, or how they would know they were done.

She and Karma came here all the time, but suddenly, the people in the graves seemed a lot deader. They seemed to be present, like each stone was really a person. Each one of them had been, to themselves, exactly what Jessy was to herself. They all saw the world as it was to who they were. And now they were under the ground, and mostly forgotten.

Suddenly Karma gasped.

"Look," she whispered intently. "It's Scott Visner's grave!"

The moonlight seemed to strike the stone special, so it sparkled in the light, the surface broken into tiny, shiny particles. The name was engraved in deep, straight letters. Twyla had known Scott, and so had Karma; he was a lot older, but they were neighbors. Scott had been killed in a car accident last summer, riding in the back of a pickup truck with some other kids, when it hit another car. He'd been really popular, on the football team, and a lot of people had been really shaken up when it happened.

Scott just stared at the marker, frozen by the sight of his own first name on the tombstone.

"Do you think he's ... really there?" Karma asked quietly.

Suddenly his presence seemed malevolent. Like he was in the earth, angry with them for being alive, for coming to the cemetery so frivolously. Nobody said anything about why, but they were all unexpectedly afraid of him.

"Maybe he's gone on to a better place," Tracy said, hesitant. "You know, this isn't really him. Not really."

"That's true," Jessy agreed. Wherever he was, he wasn't watching them. He didn't know. Probably.

"But we don't really know for sure, do we?" Tracy went on.

"Like, where his spirit really is," Jessy said.

"No," Scott said, his voice sounding strange. "We don't know where he is."

Stillness settled over them, tense, as if they were just waiting for something to jump out and scare them, to break the tension. But nothing was going to, so they were just getting more scared.

"We should go," Karma said. "Seriously."

They hadn't actually seen a ghost, or any mysterious lights, but they didn't really need to anymore. Everyone started walking just a little bit faster.

"Wait up," Jessy said. "There's something I have to do."

"I want to get out of here," Tracy said.

"It's something I have to do in private."

Everyone but Karma looked puzzled.

"Do you have to go to the bathroom or something?" Scott asked, but innocently, not like he was giving her a hard time.

"I need to commune with the spirits," she said, sort of dramatically.

Clearly, the other kids had no idea what she was talking about.

"Like with a Ouija board," Karma explained.

"We'll go on ahead," Corey said.

"But wait for us by the gate."

Once they were gone, Jessy wasn't nervous anymore. She and Karma stood for a minute, not moving, just basking in the darkness. Then they looked for a spot to bury their talisman bags.

Karma poked at a spot on the dark earth. "The ground is hard," she whispered. Jessy crouched down next to her, and tried to pry it with her fingers.

"We didn't bring anything to dig with," she said.

"Here," Karma said. They tucked the bags deep in the lower branches of a heavily overgrown evergreen bush. They were practically buried.

"Now I guess we'll see what happens."

They started down the path, toward the entrance.

"What if Johnny the Hangman were real?" Karma said.

"What do you mean?"

"Well, what if his spirit was actually here, in the cemetery? What if we pretended to call upon him, and we really did?"

"He couldn't hurt us," Jessy said. "He's already dead."

"We don't know what spirits can do. They're supernatural, remember? Preternatural."

"But Twyla just made the whole thing up," Jessy said. "Right?"

As the paved path curved and started to stare directly at the front gate, they realized they couldn't see the other kids.

"Jessy!" a big stage whisper came out of nowhere. "Karma!"

Scott and Tracy started toward them. They had ducked down the alley.

"A cop car came by," Scott said.

They walked back to the playground, Tracy and Karma a little ahead of the others, and Scott looking up at the overcast sky.

"We should meet for UFO watching again," he said. "Now that it gets darker so much earlier, they'd be easier to see. Wait -- now I don't see Troy anywhere."

"I hope she didn't get too scared," Tracy worried.

Their feet crunched loudly when they hit the sandy-surfaced part of the playground. Somebody jumped in the shadows cast by the tangle of lilac bush, and then their figures emerged.

"Hey, there you are," Tracy said. Jessy thought Troy looked sheepish. Had he and Michelle been kissing? Twyla had lots of stories about friends of hers who got caught kissing people they shouldn't, getting in trouble with their boyfriends or girlfriends.

"Did you see anything?" Troy asked.

They all looked at each other.

"No," Jessy said. "Nothing happened."

She and Karma went back to Corey's to collect their bags.

"It's getting pretty late," Corey said. "Maybe I should go in."

"You can walk with us a little longer," Jessy told her.

Karma added, "Let's see if there's any houses we missed."

Their route back in Jessy's direction took them by the Murder House again. None of the other trick-or-treaters were in sight. It had gotten a lot darker; the moon was completely smothered in dark clouds. Every house on the street seemed like it had a ghost in every window.

"We have to do it," Karma said, as they neared the Murder House. They all looked solemn. "Agreed?"

They nodded. The walkway up to the front door seemed very long, but they walked down it. They knew the house was white, but the walls looked like a faded grey. Next to the front door, a flat orange glow burned inside the plastic strip of doorbell, a will-o'-the-wisp of electricity.

They looked at each other, and finally, Jessy pushed it.

It was so quiet, they could hear the faint trill of the bell as it rang inside the empty house. Jessy realized she was holding her breath. She felt stupid for feeling scared, but at least she could say she'd done it.

There was a flare of muffled light in one of the darkened windows. Jessy was sure it was a reflection, a car down the street, but she stared intently at the glass. She couldn't see a thing.

"There's nobody home," she whispered.

"Well, we knew that," Karma whispered back.

Behind them, there was a rustling noise. It seemed to rustle more, and louder. They all turned to look, and saw the heavy evergreen branches in the bank of pines swaying, dancing back and forth. Suddenly a group of figures, Jessy couldn't tell how many, seemed to emerge from out of the darkness, like they'd always been there, but she hadn't seen them before. They were wearing hoods, and some kind of robes, and they each held something silvery in their hands, the shape of a crescent moon.

One of the girls screamed, and someone grabbed Jessy's hand, and they all ran, straight across the lawn to the sidewalk, around the corner, down the block. Karma stopped abruptly, and they all came to a confused stop. She turned back to look, and the other girls looked with her. All along the dusky-lit sidewalk, the street, it was empty.

"There's nobody there," Jessy half laughed, half out of breath.

"Geez," Corey said. "I almost had a heart attack."

"Come on," Karma said. "We'll walk you home."

They dropped her off, still giggling with fear, calling "See you Monday!"

Walking back, Jessy stared up at the dark sky behind the silent Murder House, the black trees shivering against it like shadow puppets. She inhaled deeply, as if she could breathe in the night.

"Is that?" Karma asked. She was holding out her arm, stretching her palm. "It's starting to snow."

They huddled their bags under their coats, and walked faster. It was only a few blocks, but the snow began to blur against the yellow and brown leaves, and dampen the figure hanging in Jessy's yard, its grey cloak flaring at them as they passed it.

The jack-o-lanterns still sat flickering in front of her house, bright orange eyes staring at her, like they knew everything.

Inside, the house was warm, and smelled of pumpkin and wax.

"You girls are awfully late," her mom said, while they detangled from their wings and their coats, but she didn't sound mad.

"Spooky out there tonight, huh?" her dad asked, looking at their faces. Then he glanced at their bags. "Good haul?"

"Yeah," Jessy said.

"Where's your sister?" her mom asked.

"We kind of got lost," Jessy said. "She's probably still looking for us."

At her mom's expression, she began elaborating. "It was our fault. We ran into a friend of hers, who was taking her little brother. A really little kid. They were talking, and his costume was coming apart, so we said we'd go on ahead. We went along a little too far, and we lost her."

Her mom's face looked tight, but her dad said, "Well, she'll turn up."

"You're getting to be big girls," her mom said, like she was making a big announcement. "So I'm not going to go through your candy this year." She sounded pretty uncertain about that, but kept going. "Before you eat anything, make sure to check all the wrappers. If it looks like it's been unwrapped and re-wrapped, don't eat it. Look for holes, even tiny holes. Even a pinprick."

"We'll look really carefully," Jessy promised.

"Okay, good."

Up in Jessy's room, they rolled out their sleeping bags on the floor, and plumped up their pillows to lean on. Then they poured the candy from their bags into the space between, careful to keep the contents separated from each other. They snatched out their dollar bills, and began to scrutinize.

There were legends about kids whose parents confiscated their bags, only letting them eat so much on Halloween night. They'd tuck the rest away into some kind of candy vault, and ration out the pieces. That would be horrible!

They had fat popcorn balls, in tight cellophane wrappers. Packets of the enormous SweeTart candies, a pair of them tucked inside a paper rectangle. Handfuls of taffy-like candies, twisted into orange and black waxed paper, the orange ones melty and tasting of peanut butter, the black ones soft licorice. Rolls of Smartees, which they judged according to the variety of pastel colors. Nobody liked too many of the same color in a row.

Because the word "smart" was in the name, everyone said they were candy pills, supposed to make you smarter.

"I'm going to save some for the next math test," Karma joked.

They'd gotten all sorts of bite-sized candy bars, too, and little orange suckers, with white loops of twisted paper for handles. Those had white jack-o-lanterns drawn on them; that licked right off when you sucked on them. Plus tons of Jolly Ranchers, pixie sticks, miniature Tootsie Rolls, and full-sized Tootsie Pops. That was a good candy, based on size, but the smaller suckers you could only get on Halloween, so it was a toss-up which was the superior treat.

Sugar Daddies; Bit-O-Honeys; little boxes of Milk Duds, which were fun to pick up and shake. Some kind of no-brand bubblegum, narrow pink wedges with flat ends, and the sphere-shaped lollipops that turned into a kind of powder on your tongue. How could you decide what to eat first?

Karma unwrapped one of the orange suckers, and popped the round face into her mouth. Jessy started with the Tootsie Rolls.

"We didn't imagine it, did we?" Karma asked.

"All three of us couldn't imagine it," Jessy said.

The sleet was turning more solid outside the window.

"I was just thinking about your story," Karma said. "It's weird to think of running from vampires in the snow." Then she added, "You'd know if you were dead, wouldn't you?"

"Of course you would."

"I saw this movie once, where there was a ghost, and they didn't know they were dead. They kept reliving what they were doing, the night they died."

"Everybody's heard a story about that," Jessy said.

"Yeah. It's weird that so many people think that can happen."

"Maybe we're dead right now," Jessy joked.

"Don't say that," Karma said. "It's bad luck."

Before they went to sleep, they gathered their candy together again. Karma shoved her bag between the sleeping bag and the wall, and Jessy set hers on the desk, in a nest of paper.

In the middle of the night, Jessy half woke up, as if she'd heard something. Her door was open a crack, when she was sure she'd left if as closed as it would go. It looked like a shadow in the doorway, and in the darkness, she thought it was Twyla, looking in. Jessy started to sit up to say something, but there was no one there.

She must have just come in from the party, she thought. But then she was startled by a thought. Karma said it happened all the time, that ghosts visited people, right when they died. What if something had happened to Twyla, right that second, like the ghost in the story? She looked over at Karma, who was obviously sound asleep, and then she put her head back on the pillow, turned toward the door, closing her eyes almost all the way.

She waited. There was another faint sound, a creak. The door opened slightly wider. A figure stepped, silent, into the room. Jessy tried not to make a sound. It really was Twyla. She stepped toward the desk, and then she reached carefully into the bag and grabbed a piece of candy.

****

Saturday, November 1

In the morning, fat clumps of wet white fuzz stuck in the grass. The pumpkins wore small white hats, just covering the bald spots on the tops of their heads.

"I don't know what time she got in," her mom was saying. "And I don't know how much more we can ground her."

"Good morning, girls," her dad broke in cheerily, when he saw her and Karma in the doorway.

They ate pancakes and drank cocoa, and eventually Jessy's mom demanded that she go upstairs and get her sister out of bed right this minute. Jessy knocked on the door a couple of times, and then pushed it open.

Twyla moaned lightly when she turned to look at her, but her voice sounded pretty normal.

"Good haul?" she asked.

"Yeah," Jessy said. "And we went to the cemetery."

Twyla sat up, making room for Jessy to sit on the bed.

"Did you see any lights?"

"No. The police came by, though. So I think it was a police car that those kids saw. If they saw anything at all."

"Did you run into any Moonies?" To anyone else, Twyla would have sounded completely straight-faced, but Jessy could hear the tiny echo of teasing.

"No, we didn't," she said, trying to keep equally serious.

"I heard that they were skulking around, looking for kids to kidnap."

Twyla would definitely get in more trouble than she did, if she ever sounded that obvious to their Mom. Jessy knew, and Twyla knew that she knew, and she knew that she knew that she knew. So Twyla threw her covers off, and climbed off the foot of the bed to dig in the pile of heaped-up jackets. She pulled out a stick, with a foil curve of crescent moon glued onto it.

"It wasn't hard to talk anybody into scaring little kids," she said. "We had a lot of fun with it. I was just afraid you weren't going to show up. There was a keg out at Johnson's Farm, so we couldn't stay out all night."

The stairs creaked with someone coming upstairs, and in a minute, their Mom appeared in the doorway.

"I'm really sick," Twyla said. The moon hidden; her voice instantly raspy. "My throat really hurts. I must have gotten a chill last night."

Their mom made a slight "hmph" noise. Jessy went downstairs with her, and when they passed the flaming skull decoration at the bottom of the stairs, her mom said "All this stuff is coming down on Monday."

Jessy had already hidden the pop-up cat in her closet, to protect it from going into the Jack-o-Lantern Box.

After breakfast they took the piñata to Karma's, and tied it to the clothesline where their pretend Johnny had claimed his first victim. The patches of snow had completely faded away. They found a couple of old brooms in the garage, and checked their weight, smacking the sides into their palms, like billy clubs. Then they took turns bashing him.

Several hits, and the paper-mache started to bend, like an egg at the moment of cracking. Johnny's side gashed open. Karma gave it one last strong whack, and he was completely crushed -- nothing left but the skin of paper-mache and a pulp of orange tissue paper.

"Johnny's really dead, now," Karma said.

"Until next Halloween," Jessy added. "When his ghost will walk again."

When she got home, she caught her dad out by the garbage cans, throwing away a bundle of the Indian corn from his workshop. It had clearly been gnawed on.

"Don't tell your mom about this," he said.

That night, Jessy got her notebook out, and wrote the word "Hobgoblin" partway down the first page, in pen, like it was the title page of a real book. She had an idea for a story about a Hobgoblin Party. Someone would find the *Orange and Black Book*, and follow the instructions, and doing that would wake up the ghosts who had read the book years ago. Maybe it would cause whatever happened in the past to happen again, to new people.

She thought about what Karma had said, about ghosts who kept reliving their lives. Then she thought, if you were a ghost, walking in and out of the same place for decades, wouldn't you notice that the rooms had changed?

Maybe every time was still taking place, like yesterday was still going on somewhere, and tomorrow was happening. If you were a ghost, maybe you could travel between them. Maybe you wouldn't even notice.

It might be just like playing make-believe. That wasn't hard.

The problem was: how did you know when you were a ghost, and when the world was real? Right now, her room was stable, inside the old house's firm wooden walls, but for all she knew, it could dissolve into mist at any moment.

It wasn't always even death that made things change. She and Karma talked about going to college and getting an apartment, and some of their friends had already planned their weddings -- what kind of gowns, how many bridesmaids. Even if Twyla didn't run away to become a rock star, she was going to graduate in another year. They weren't all going to live in this house forever.

Part of Jessy didn't even want to think about it, but maybe she could turn it into a story.

It was already dark outside: November. Halloween was over. Before long, it was going to be Thanksgiving, and then Christmas.

The pumpkins would shrivel up, around their eyes and mouths first, and then the lids would start to shrink. Stacks of leaves would drift up, scatter and then pile up again, until the whole earth was covered over, if they didn't rake them.

She and Twyla and Karma and everybody she knew were eventually going to blow off the trees, blow away down the street. They were ghosts and cobwebs. All the wet leaves crumbled back down into the earth, and they were beautiful.

About the Author

   Karen Joan Kohoutek grew up in Wadena, Minnesota, and now lives in Fargo, North Dakota, where she is known for her annual library program, Ghost Stories for Grown-Ups. In ten years, the themes have included "Dark Carnival," "When the Hearse Goes By," and "Thesaurus of Horror." She has also appeared different times in the *Fargo Forum* as a local expert on ghost stories and horror movies. In 2002, she received a Master of Fine Arts in Creative Writing from Minnesota State University Moorhead. She lives with her like-minded husband and two Halloween tabbies (grey and orange).

   You can visit her online at octoberzine.blogspot.com, or contact her at octoberzine@gmail.com.

www.ingramcontent.com/pod-product-compliance
Lightning Source LLC
Chambersburg PA
CBHW031842170626
46807CB00004B/1579